SINFUL ENFORCER

MAFIA MISFITS BOOK 6

ASIA MONIQUE

SYNOPSIS

Gaia Wilson

I wanted nothing to do with him.

His eyes were lifeless.

His demeanor cold.

His actions too harsh.

Ricardo Carter wasn't the kind of man you fell in love with, he was the kind you ran from.

Ricardo "Rocco" Carter

I wanted everything to do with her.

Her eyes were full of life.

Her demeanor soft.

Her actions thoughtful.

Gaia Wilson was the kind of woman you fell in love with, she was the kind you ran toward.

Note: *Sinful Enforcer is book six in the mafia misfits series and can be read as a standalone. This story includes depictions of violence; may be sensitive for some readers.*

INTRODUCTION

Hey, book whores!

I know you've been waiting on this one. Thank you to everyone who was patient with me while I took a break after writing 45 books in four years—back to back—but also, as I followed where my heartstrings were pulling me, once I came back with *'And Then Life Was Beautiful'*.

I understand that when a series starts you expect the author to continue with it until it has concluded, but as a creator of words and worlds I will always go where the creativity leads me.

With that being said, I hope you enjoy this slightly chaotic but beautiful ride Gaia and Rocco are about to take you on. It'll be nothing like you expected it to be.

xoxo, Asia Monique

FAMILY TREE

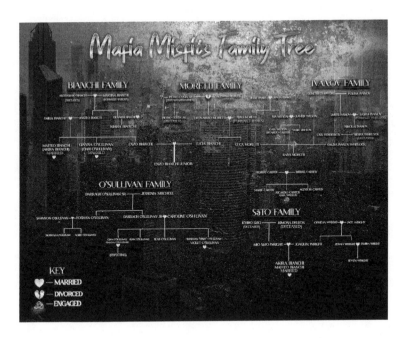

TRIGGER WARNINGS

Sexual abuse (discussed)
Emotional and mental abuse
Manipulative/elitist parents
Adoption
This story includes depictions of violence; may be sensitive for some readers.

PROLOGUE

LUCIA MORETTI

THE SET UP...

"Why am I getting the feeling this is a setup?" Gaia asked, her eyes moving from me to Enzo and back. "Whatever the two of you are up to, I want no parts."

"*We* aren't up to shit," Enzo said from where he stood. "Argue with your girl, not me."

He ambled over and took our almost one month old from my arms.

"You're supposed to have my back," I muttered into his ear as he kissed my cheek.

Enzo chuckled and murmured back, "No. Playing matchmaker with my wife was never part of our plans."

"We've never exactly stuck to any of our plans, so what's one more time?"

He stepped back and I peered up at him from my seat on the sofa.

1

Enzo as a father was a sight to behold.

The way he cared for our son made me want to give him more babies sometime soon, just not yet. I was ready to get back to work and it was driving me crazy that I had to take time off to heal. Playing a little matchmaker with my cousin would keep me occupied for a while.

What better way to spend my time healing then by pairing the notoriously calm mafia enforcer and a soft hearted lover girl with murderous tendencies.

"Two things can be true at once, *Bellissima*," Enzo said, drawing me from my thoughts.

"Stop talking about me in code like I'm not standing here listening," Gaia complained.

Enzo dipped low, our son perched on his chest with one hand, and kissed my forehead.

"I'll leave you to deal with her. Don't overdo yourself up here while I'm gone."

He turned and walked toward Gaia, stopping to peer down at her with a smirk on his face.

"Maybe, don't kill Rocco while the two of you are away," he mused, laughter in his voice. "He'd probably let you if you asked, so don't."

I waited until Enzo was in the elevator and the doors were closed to address Gaia again.

"I do need you on this job," I said, patting the empty space beside me.

She huffed but took up residence where I'd requested without a fight.

"What's in the DMV that's so important to you and Enzo?" she asked, lifting a perfectly arched brow. "And why can't you send Violet or Jaz?"

"Violet is stalking her admirer and Jaz accepted two

contracts recently; furthermore, only you can help Rocco in the way he needs."

"So, there's actually a job that needs to be done? This isn't just you playing matchmaker?"

A little white lie wouldn't hurt, right?

"Enzo wants to know who his father's biological family is," I revealed, telling a partial truth. "We were able to pin down some records that were sealed. He was born somewhere in the DMV."

"Does Angelo know the two of you are meddling?"

I shook my head.

"Enzo has been curious since we found out I was pregnant and now that our son is here, the man is relentless in his quest."

It probably wouldn't end well, but he and I were prepared for the fallout.

"I can dig into this from here, Luci."

"Sure but we have other leads that require in person investigation," I explained, slipping my lie in to seal the deal. "Rocco is good with sniffing out information and with your help he could do it faster. Plus, he's from D.C. and knows the surrounding areas better than anyone."

Gaia rolled her eyes but I knew she would agree.

"Enzo corrupted you," she accused. "Now that you believe in love you can't help but want it for the rest of us. I need you to know that Rocco is not my person."

"I've always believed in love," I reminded her. "Enzo only made me realize I'd lost my way, that's all. Maybe you need a reminder of what could be."

She fell back into the sofa and sighed.

"Luci, I'm happy for you. I even sorta kinda like Enzo because he's good to you, but falling in love is not on my agenda right now. Especially, not with that psychotic ass man."

Rocco was the most reasonable between him, Enzo, and Matteo.

How couldn't she see that?

"What happened when you were with him before?" I asked, turning my body to face hers.

"Nothing. He's simply not my kind of guy."

She was a bad fucking liar but I knew how to get Gaia talking.

"Okay..." I shrugged and stood. "But you do need some dick, so how about you use him for that."

I moved around the living room, gathering all the shit that had accumulated since the day started.

"Don't start cleaning after suggesting that. I can't fuck that man for fun and you know it."

She followed me up the hall and into the baby's room.

"Lucia, do not ignore me. You know how much I hate it."

I dumped the mess I'd collected on the changing table and started to sort through it.

"Fine!" she exclaimed after I continued to ignore her. "I'll tell you, even though there's really nothing to tell."

I turned after schooling the smile on my face.

She'd been keeping what happened the first time her and Rocco were in D.C. together close to the chest. He'd done or said something to send her running for the hills.

"Before you start, will this make me hate him?"

Rocco was such a likeable guy; it would break my heart to have to kill him, but I would.

"I really wish I could say yes to that..." Gaia leaned into the door frame and crossed her arms. "No, you won't hate him. He didn't do anything specific."

I frowned.

"So, there isn't actually a problem."

She returned the frown, hers more out of frustration than mine.

"He's the problem, Lucia."

"Why?"

"Have you ever looked in his eyes before? There's nothing there. When we brought those girls here, he didn't bat an eye. He wasn't angry or disgusted or any fucking thing. His smile isn't real. That carefree attitude isn't either. He's like a walking robot and I need a walking man with feelings. Don't get me wrong the man is beautiful but I can't do it."

I regarded her closely while mentally running down all of the encounters I'd had with Rocco this year. How I saw Rocco was nothing like she'd described.

He cared.

He had feelings and a family he loved.

Rocco was so much more than what meets the eye.

I got to learn those intimate details because he allowed me to.

Gaia had pegged the man wrong or maybe she saw something only *he* was allowing her to see. In which case, I needed to fallback.

"I understand," I said, nodding. "You don't have to go but he could still use your help. Maybe set up one of those secure chat lines for him to use and go from there."

"This is important to you and Enzo, right?"

"It is, but like I said--"

"I'll go as long as we have an understanding that there will be no Gaia and Ricardo."

I threw my hands up in surrender.

"No Gaia and *Ricardo.* Got it."

Gaia Juliette Wilson was a horrible liar.

PART ONE
"HIS TRUE NATURE OPENED MY HEART AND MY LEGS."

- Gaia Wilson

CHAPTER 1
GAIA WILSON

Before leaving town, it was imperative I stopped by my parent's home in Philly to let them know I'd be gone for a while. My dad required it and I had no problem obliging; this life was dangerous enough and he was my biggest protector.

"Hey, Dad. Are you in here?"

I knocked on the shed's door and then poked my head inside.

My father stood in front of a body suspended in the air, his hands on his hips.

"Come look at this, Munchkin," he beckoned. "Do you think he had sickle cell?"

I stepped beside him and observed the man with his eyes pried open.

"Possibly. Or a liver issue. Why?"

He poked an eye with his gloved finger and the man flinched, showing signs of life.

"Dad, what did he do?"

"Popped his shit about being the new big man in town," he

9

mused, pulling his gloves off. "Had to remind him and everyone else that I'm the only man with power around here."

"Don't you think it's time to let all of this go?" I asked, meeting the eyes of a monster I loved deeply.

He smiled, his lips curling menacingly.

My father had worked hard to get his version of a loving grin down. I'd grown to love and understand it over the years.

Xavier Wilson hadn't been capable of love until he met my mother. It was when I came along that he'd presented signs of being a man with feelings.

At least that's how my mother explained it.

"There's nothing to let go off, Munchkin..." He looked at his watch. "I have a meeting across town, did you need me for something?"

He tipped his head for me to follow him and I obliged, trailing his broad frame toward the main house.

"I just came to let you and mama know that I'll be out of town for a little while. Not sure how long but I'm hoping only a week or two."

He led us in through the back door, straight into the state of the art kitchen he'd built for my mother.

Nia Wilson turned and her soft eyes brightened at the sight of me.

"Hey, babygirl," she greeted, kissing both of my cheeks. "What brings you this way?"

"She's going out of town..." My father's narrowed eyes met mine from where he stood. "Though, she doesn't exactly want to go."

I scoffed and opened the fridge to give myself time to think.

"I hate when you read me that way," I griped. "I agreed to help Luci with something, it's not a big deal."

I turned to face my parents, who stood one in front of the other.

My dad had his arms around her from behind, his chin atop her head.

She looked happy and in love even after almost thirty years together.

Their love for another was evident.

"It's a big deal when my daughter has fear dancing in her eyes. That's an emotion I don't appreciate seeing from one of my favorite girls."

"I—dad, I'm not afraid of anyone. Not in the way you think, at least."

"Ah, so some man has your attentio—ah, shit."

He released my mother after she elbowed him in the gut.

"I'm proud of that stiff elbow, Nia."

His knowing gaze bore into mine as he caressed his abdomen.

My mom took steps toward me, her eyes filled with understanding.

"Xavier, give me a moment with Gaia."

"I'll be upstairs getting ready for my meeting," he conceded, pressing a kiss to both our foreheads before retreating.

"Come sit," she ordered, leading us to the enclosed nook surrounded by large bay windows.

"Ma, I don't need a—"

"Close your mouth and open your ears. You need to hear this."

I nodded and placed my hand in hers.

"I know you see your father and it's hard to comprehend how someone like him can be a family man. But his version of love is also mine and that's how we work. You have to dig deep within to find yours. Don't look at me and your father or the love lives of your cousins as reference. What's for them may not be for you."

Her fingers tightened around mine as she regarded me closely.

"What's this internal battle you're having?"

I looked away.

"I don't know if I'm capable of this life anymore. The things I've seen don't go away."

Sleep evaded me most nights.

Who I was becoming terrified me at times, but I couldn't bring myself to stop.

"Dad didn't choose this life, he adopted it to survive," I went on. "Luca and Lucia were bred to be who they are. I made a choice and maybe part of me is starting to regret it."

"Choices were made, you're right..." She gripped my chin and I met her challenging gaze. "Everything you start, you can stop."

"I know."

Nothing was ever that simple though.

Stopping meant turning my back on the family, on the mafia.

Part of me wasn't sure what I wanted or why I was struggling this badly as of late.

The things I'd done and seen hadn't scared me. Not once had I batted an eye.

Until *him*.

All of my insecurities started after I looked into his cold eyes and saw a glimpse of the future—one where my eyes mirrored his.

Cold.

Dark.

Empty.

But so full of love somewhere deep within them.

I couldn't imagine losing who I am at the core for love.

"I have to head out..." I stood and pulled her with me. "I need to go on a run and clear my head, can't do that on jobs."

She cupped my face and drew my forehead to her lips.

"I love you, my sweet girl," she murmured, releasing me after. "You've always been soft at heart. I know you hide it for good reason but maybe that part of you needs refuge somewhere safe. Trust yourself."

I nodded.

"Yes, ma'am. Always listen to my gut, I know."

She kissed me again and led me to the door where my father was waiting, dressed in a Tom Ford suit.

"You look good, papa bear!"

He turned with a grin on his face.

"Please, don't give the man a big head."

"A big head never hurt nobody, Nia," he quipped, tugging me into his side. "Be safe out there, Munchkin. Call if you need me."

"I'll call if I want bloodshed."

We migrated from the house onto the front lawn as a dark colored sedan rolled to a stop in the middle of the street.

"Is that Yasir?"

Dad opened my car door and waved for me to get in.

"That's him," he said. "He's on my bad side this week, so don't expect your favorite cousin to get out and speak."

I rolled my eyes and slid into the driver's seat.

"He's always on your bad side. Stop testing him and he won't challenge you back. Yasir is the only worthy replacement as the Kings leader."

"My daughter could also be that worthy replacement," he mused, eyeing me closely.

"I'm not the person you want as leader of a street gang, Dad. Let's be foreal here. Yasir was bred for this. Uncle Ya made sure of it when you and ma didn't have more kids. Stop being a stubborn Wilson man and remind your nephew that you love him and you're proud. Sometimes all we need is a reminder."

He leaned in and braced his hands on the top of the car.

"I not only love you but I'm proud of the woman you've become, Munchkin."

My stomach fluttered and I beamed at him.

"I love you, too, Dad. Thank you for telling me that."

He tapped the hood and dipped his head in response before shutting my door.

My father knew when I needed to hear his love for me through words, but I'd meant it when I said Yasir might've needed it too.

He was tough, my cousin, but he'd lost his father at a pentacle point in a teenage boy's life.

His mother never recovered from losing the love of her life to the streets.

Yasir lived with us up until we both moved out in our early twenties.

I grabbed my phone as I bent the corner and dialed Yasir.

"Knew you'd call," he said upon answering.

"Just checking on my favorite cousin."

He chuckled.

"I thought Luca was your favorite."

"He's my favorite when I'm with him and vice versa."

Yasir and Luca were like oil and water and avoided one another like the plague.

It was best for both their well-being.

"Dad is only hard on you because of what happened to Uncle Ya. He won't survive another loss like that."

"I know, G."

"Good. He loves you and so do I."

I could hear my father's deep baritone in the background, followed by a door shutting.

"Gotta go, G. I love you, too."

Yasir ended the call and another came through soon after from Galina, Luca's fiancée.

They were marrying in the spring after she gave birth to their daughter in March.

"Hey, my love," I greeted after syncing my phone to the car's stereo.

"Are you okay?" she asked, throwing me off. "You don't have to answer that but I was thinking about you and felt the urge to call and ask."

"I don't know..." I shrugged as if she could see me and merged onto the beltway. "There's a lot on my mind."

She hummed, her mind working up possible solutions to my problem.

"Luca said you would be in D.C. for a while. I can stop by and water your plants while you're away."

I sighed, grateful for her sweet nature.

Galina and Luca lived only a few townhomes down from me and we spent a lot of our free time together.

"I appreciate you for thinking of my babies, but I'd rather not hear your beasts mouth about having you do manual labor while pregnant."

She scoffed.

"I can handle my beast just fine. Luca doesn't get a say on how I spend my pregnancy. Not when I'm carrying this big ass baby for him. Six months, Gaia! I'm six months and I've gained so much weight."

"Now, Doc. Let's be foreal."

"Fine," she grumbled. "My weight gain isn't what I'm making it seem, but this baby is big and labor is going to be brutal. I need to stay moving to make it easier on me. Plus, I want to snap back quick to fit into my wedding dress."

I chuckled.

She was stressed about that damn dress.

"At least drive to my front door," I reasoned. "No walking. I know the weather is playing tricks on us right now but it's still winter."

"Twice a week, right? I'll do it after work."

I rolled my car to a stop outside our gated community, keyed in my personal code and drove through.

"Great," I griped as I turned into my driveway.

"That didn't sound like a response to me."

"It wasn't. I have an unwanted guest."

Ricardo pushed his bulky frame off the back of his Camaro.

My stomach fluttered at the sight of him and I cursed.

"Should I call Luc--"

"No, it's okay," I cut in, removing my seatbelt. "I can handle it. Thank you for calling to check on me."

"Of course. Call if you need anything."

I tapped the end button on my steering wheel and leaned back in my seat.

He couldn't see me through my illegal tint but stared into the windshield, his emotionless eyes pinned to where I sat, as if he could.

I'd been raised by a scary man, shared blood with a mafia boss and a goddamn assassin.

My friend group consisted of nothing but gun toting murderous women.

I'd never been a scary bitch but for the first time in my life, something scared me--*someone* scared me.

My heart raced.

My skin tingled with awareness.

The hairs on the back of my neck stood tall and at attention.

Ricardo *fucking* Carter.

CHAPTER 2
RICARDO CARTER

Enzo pointed to the gift box I set in front of him.

"What's that?"

"Something I picked up for little man..." I dropped into a chair and slid down. "Actually, my sister sent it and I put my name next to hers on the card."

Had the card already been sealed when it arrived at my doorstep? *Sure.*

But what my sister didn't know, wouldn't come back to haunt me.

Enzo flicked the top off and peered inside, slowly leaning forward in an attempt not to wake the miniature version of himself sleeping on his chest.

Seeing Enzo as a dad was mind boggling to say the least.

We'd done some fucked up shit over the years, especially back when he didn't have a team of men doing his bidding. Back when I was the only man outside of Matteo willing to tag along and handle the dirty shit a sane man would never want to touch.

"Fucking Ree..." He pulled a Temple University debate team

t-shirt with baby Enzo's name scrawled on the back from the box. "Always politicking for somebodies baby to be a goddamn lawyer."

I shrugged.

Being on the debate team was my father's way of preparing us to be great lawyers.

My sisters loved it but I had no interest in yelling over a room full of people to get my point across, not when shooting the place up held more weight in my eyes.

"Family business," I reminded him.

Enzo nodded and leaned back, regarding me in a way only he could.

"Why are you really here, Rocco? It ain't to give me this shirt from your sister."

"Needed to get your blessing on something," I said, sitting up. "Before I head to D.C."

His eyes were knowing as he said, "You mean before you get to spend six uninterrupted weeks with Gaia."

"Does she know that? How long we'll be gone?"

Enzo moved his namesake from one shoulder to the other, his gaze unwavering.

I'd never been easy to read.

He despised that about me, most people did.

"She doesn't but you're going to tell her the moment she's in your purview."

"That an order, Boss?"

He chuckled and leaned back, his gaze following the gentle strokes of his fingertips up and down baby Enzo's back.

"I love this little boy," he said, shaking his head. "He's what I've always wanted. Lucia is the only person I can see myself with in this lifetime..." He looked up. "You've never wanted this, Roc. Why now?"

The answer was simple.

"Why not now? I'm allowed to change my mind."

I wasn't easily swayed into doing so, but the decision had been all mine.

"You are..." He nodded. "So, let me ask this, why *her*?"

"Never really cared about how people view me..." I looked away, unsure of how I was feeling but certain it all went back to the moment I met Gaia. "I might care about how she sees me though."

Before Enzo could hound me for a more detailed response, Lucia came bustling into his office and he stood to greet her.

"I would like to have cuddles with our son now."

"He'll be squirming soon for food anyway," Enzo said as they made the transfer. "I'm coming up when I'm done with Rocco."

Lucia cut her eyes my way at the mention of my name.

"Ricardo," she sang, her eyes filled with amusement.

I raised an eyebrow and she chuckled.

Lucia had never called me by my first name and her sudden use of it felt like an inside joke I wanted to be in on.

"Be good while you're away. Gaia isn't like me."

I stood and she approached, stopping directly in front of me.

"I don't see it," she murmured, staring into my eyes.

"See what?"

Lucia blinked and took a step back.

"Nothing. Be good and don't let anything happen to her."

She left without a backward glance and I turned my attention to Enzo.

"Got any clue what that was about?"

"Nope..." He moved past me and I followed him into the hall. "Even if I did, I wouldn't tell you. This is your mountain to climb. You want Gaia, work for it."

"Do I need to remind you of how you and Lucia became engaged?"

We backed away from one another.

"I know how I got my wife."

He smirked.

"And I know how to get mine," I retorted. "You just be ready for the wrath of Angelo when he finds out what we're up to."

Enzo stopped his backward pursuit and I did the same.

"You think it's a bad idea?"

"Personally, no. Will your pops feel a way, for sure."

He nodded.

"It's happening regardless. He'll get over it."

"You got over what he did," I pointed out. "Common courtesy is him returning the favor."

"Maybe work shit out with your pops while you're there," he tossed out as he retreated.

His suggestion left a nasty taste in my mouth.

My father was a man I tolerated and for the sake of keeping the relationships I had with my mother and two sisters intact, it would stay that way.

We had a routine.

I stayed away until my mother demanded my presence.

He texted on birthdays and I sent my well wishes via third party as a show of respect.

It was better that way, us living separate lives.

There was an unspoken rule that had me reaching for my phone and calling my mother.

As I settled into the driver's seat of my car, she picked up.

"Does this phone call mean you'll be in town soon?" she asked upon answering. "I hope so because your father's birthday is approaching and our annual gala falls on the same day."

I let her get what she'd probably been waiting to tell me for weeks off her chest, listening intently for the underlying message.

My father's birthday was on New Year's day--less than a week away.

"You won't miss it this year for obvious reasons," she went on.

"We've talked about this," I reminded her. "I won't be attending, same as the last six years."

"Ricardo..." She sighed. "This has to stop. You and your father, this distance between the family. You being in New Jersey doing God knows what."

I didn't have it in me to work up a defense.

The weight on my shoulders to fix an unfixable relationship was heavy.

Fuck how I felt about his treatment toward me.

Fuck him being the parent in this dynamic.

It was all on me.

"I'll be in town for a few weeks," I told her, starting my car. "Set up a lunch or dinner with you, Ree, and Ally. Doesn't matter the day, I'll make time for it."

"And the party?"

"You know the answer already. I won't change my mind."

Disappointing her was becoming the new normal for our relationship.

It was a sad affair, for her and me.

I loved my mother and sisters, but our lives simply didn't mix.

"Alright," she said softly. "I'll take what I can get. Your sisters will be happy to see you."

"Not you?"

"Of course me, Ricardo. You're my baby. No matter what."

Didn't feel that way, never had to be truthful.

"Yeah, no matter what," I muttered, backing out of my parking spot. "I have to go get myself together for my flight out tonight."

"I can send the jet if you—"

"I have one chartered already, but I'll see you soon. I love you."

I had to let her go before she circled back to the original conversation.

My mother wasn't the kind of woman who gave up easily. She convinced people to do exactly what she wanted for a living and made no qualms about using those techniques on her children.

When you grow up in the environment I did, it sticks with you.

It shaped you.

It shaped me, at least.

I am who I am because of them.

And the only way to get *her* to understand me is to show her who I am at the core.

Taking Gaia to D.C. was the first step in that.

"About time you got here," Matteo complained from my sofa as I entered my apartment. "Let Akira give you the pep talk she's been working on and we'll be out of your hair."

He rested back and lifted his boot clad feet onto my coffee table.

I'd known they were here after spotting the midnight black Maserati in the parking garage.

This had become a thing for Matteo and his wife Akira, moving in twos.

They never left each other's side unless business demanded it.

"Have some fucking manners, Matteo," Akira fussed,

making her presence known after poking her head out the kitchen archway.

"Hey, Rocco. Come talk to me."

She dipped back into the kitchen and I glanced at Matteo, who watched me expectantly.

"Is hearing her out a direct order?" I asked, prepared to walk right past the kitchen.

He chuckled.

"Fuck, no. But if you offend her, then I'll be offended. It'll become a thing and you know I hate those."

He waved his hand, as if what he said convinced me that the conversation was necessary.

It wasn't.

"The faster you let her theories about your love life fill those big ears of yours, the quicker we'll be out of your locs. Wake me when she's finished."

"Don't listen to him," Akira said while peeling an orange. "I don't have a theory, plural or otherwise about your love life. Who am I to talk? I almost let the love of my life go because of my own shit."

She popped an orange slice in her mouth and regarded me closely from where she stood.

My apartment wasn't anything to write home about, just a two bedroom two bathroom sparsely decorated space I called my own for most of the year.

I lived modestly in Jersey for more reasons than one.

"I'm listening," I said, leaning against the counter. "What's so important that you and your husband broke into my place?"

She smiled.

"He has a key, you know?"

"For emergencies," I reminded her.

Akira's eyes sparkled with mischief.

She was bad, this one.

The type who liked to get into trouble on purpose.

"I think you're a great guy, Rocco," she said, holding an orange slice out to me.

I reluctantly took it, eyeing the piece longer than needed.

"I wouldn't dare poison you. Not with an orange, at least. They're too good to waste that way."

She popped another in her mouth and nodded.

I dropped it in the trash, not because I didn't trust Akira but because I hated oranges.

"Who brings their own fruit to a break in?"

She chuckled and then sighed.

"I was hungry but wanted to stop by and give you this first."

Akira lifted a medium sized gift bag from the floor and set it on the counter.

"What's that?"

"The key to winning her father over," she mused, her lips curling. "He'll be your biggest challenge and I figured I'd help you with him."

She shrugged.

"Her father someone important?"

"Oh wow, Rocco. You must really be into her if you haven't dug into her life yet."

I shrugged and eyed the bag, my curiosity piqued.

"What is it?"

"You won't understand without me revealing who he is."

"I'm listening..." I rounded the counter and closed the distance between us. "I'll learn about him eventually."

"Are you sure?"

"Certain..." I tipped my head toward the bag. "Show me."

Akira removed what looked like a square-shaped suede necklace box and I frowned.

"You want me to give him jewelry?"

I personally never wore anything but watches; Some men enjoyed a chain or two or five. Not my cup of tea but I never judged.

"No, crazy. I want to give him information."

She flipped it open and inside was a single piece of paper with a name on it.

"You've heard of the South Philly Kings, right?"

I lifted an eyebrow.

"Who hasn't?"

They were a ruthless street gang no smart organization wanted to go up against.

Contrary to belief, going to war wasn't the goal of the mafia. If it didn't make money, then it didn't make sense.

"And the man in charge shares a last name with your girl," she informed me. "Xavier Wilson. He's known for having no soul, but I know he loves his family, especially his only child."

Forcing the Kings out back when Lucia's father first started making waves wouldn't have done his plans any good.

He'd been smart to stay out of their way.

"From what I know things are heating up in South Philly," Akira went on, filling me in on all she knew. "Xavier is about to step down and pass the reins to his nephew Yasir, but the whispers are saying he's waiting until their problem is neutralized."

"Mmm," I hummed as she shut the jewelry box. "Appreciate the one up but I don't need it. Pass this along to him discreetly instead."

Akira looked slightly disappointed but agreed to do as I requested.

"Sure, I can do that."

"Hey..." I reached over and gripped her shoulder gently. "I meant it when I said I appreciate this, and you for that matter, but I have to do this my way or it won't work."

She nodded slowly, her eyes thoughtful.

"I understand completely and will pass this along to someone who'll get it to her father."

"Good..." I turned to leave the kitchen. "Now take your snoring ass husband out my place before I stuff something in his mouth."

"Do that and you won't make it out of this apartment," Matteo grumbled.

I'd already made it half way up the hall to my bedroom, leaving him, his wife, and that sad ass threat where they were.

"Lock my shit up with that key I gave for emergencies only," I tossed over my shoulder before shutting my bedroom door.

"We love you, too, Ricardo!" Akira yelled back, giving me pause.

Why the fuck was everyone suddenly calling me Ricardo?

I shook off my irritation and ambled into my closet where I had one suitcase already opened and filled. Where Gaia and I were staying for the next six weeks didn't require me to pack my whole life, but before zipping it I took a shower with the few essentials left to pack.

An hour later, I found myself in the driveway of *her* home as she pulled in behind me.

I knew she wouldn't expect me this early, or at all if Gaia had anything to do with it, but I planned for just that.

For us to meet exactly like this.

I could sense her labored breaths, even with the tint in her windows blocking my view of her. My elbows connected with the hood of my car and I leaned into it, my gaze focused on the windshield, almost sure I was looking directly into Gaia's eyes.

For a moment there was no movement and I wondered how long she'd leave me standing here, but as the thought came, Gaia opened her door, and it went.

Her curly top came into view first and then flashes of her ochre skin before she turned and dipped briefly into the car again, returning with a book bag moments later. She moved around the door before shutting it, and then blessed me with every inch of her athletic stature to obsess over.

She was an avid runner and it showed in the definition of her legs and calves.

I admired the soft curves and dips she possessed, more like I obsessed over them as I worked my gaze up her otherwise petite frame. Something about her... about the way she carried herself when walking into a room full of people had done me in over the last year.

Heads turned at the sight of her--mine had more than once.

But that confidence she had with everyone else seemed to waver when I was near.

Nevertheless, she was beautiful.

Even if I scared her a little bit.

Gaia *fucking* Wilson.

She'll love me when this was all said and done.

I was sure of it.

CHAPTER 3
GAIA

"Why are you here?" I asked, moving between our two cars to stand in front of him. "I thought we didn't leave for another few hours."

I so badly needed to go for a run.

Rocco leaned back slightly and dropped his gaze, slowly moving it up my frame. The expression in his eyes didn't change, and it unnerved me. I had no idea what he was thinking and switched my body weight from one foot to the other, forcing my nervous energy away.

His gaze snapped to mine at my sudden movement.

"Figured we could leave earlier than planned..." He reached into his pocket and pulled a set a keys from it. "I arranged a secured track for your runs."

What?

"How do you know I--"

"Common knowledge," he cut in, pushing off the hood of his car and into my personal space. "We'll be gone a while. Pack heavy."

"Heavy..." His woodsy cologne stole my thoughts. "Can you back up a little?"

The expression in his eyes held a hint of defiance, but Ricardo took that step back without question and I could breathe again.

"How long is a while?" I asked, moving toward my front door.

His heavy footfalls echoed loudly as he followed.

Everything about him stood out; he never needed to speak because his presence did it for him.

"Six weeks," he murmured, talking in that low tone he used often. "Is it cool if I come in?"

I twisted the key after pushing it into the lock and glanced over my shoulder.

"I wouldn't make you sit out here while I got myself together but thank you for asking anyway."

Our eyes met briefly, but I looked away before they could linger for too long.

"You can make yourself comfortable down here. I have a lot of snacks in the kitchen, help yourself but don't touch my strawberry shortcakes."

I was already half way up the stairs by the time I finished my spiel, wanting to be hospitable but not exactly friendly.

Once behind my closed bedroom door, I dropped my bags and took a deep breath.

"*Fuck*," I grumbled.

This was going to be a goddamn disaster.

I pushed away the worry growing in the pit of my stomach and started to pack half of my closet. Six weeks was a long time without having a variety of options, and while I had bank accounts filled with money I didn't buy frivolous things while on jobs.

Two of my extra-large Beis suitcases were able to fit my

wardrobe, shoes, and essentials. I filled my weekender bag with all of my tech stuff, checking it twice to be sure I had everything I'd need to work efficiently.

I spent a short time braiding my hair down, showering, and re-dressing in a loose fitting Nike sweatsuit. It was my favorite to wear when traveling, especially in the winter.

Before I was finished a knock at my bedroom door reminded me that I had guest waiting for me.

"Sorry, I--*Oh*, it's you."

Luca walked in without speaking.

"Thought you'd be running until I saw two cars outside," he said, lifting the handles on my suitcases. "You need all this shit?"

Rolling my eyes, I went into the bathroom.

"For six weeks, yeah." I pinned my four plaits back and put a scully on. "I planned to run but I guess plans changed when I got home and Ricardo was here. What brought you by?"

Leaning into the bathroom doorframe, I watched my cousin watch me.

He was waiting for me to tell him I was good, but I wasn't so sure that I was, and we didn't lie to one another.

Luca and I *never* lied to one another.

"We should talk when you get back," he spoke after a short while of silence, nodding as if he figured me out. "I'll take these down for you."

"Thanks. I just need another minute or two. Could you let Ricardo know?"

He turned and lifted an eyebrow.

"Y'all on a government name basis?"

"No..." I walked into my closet while chastising myself for not calling him Rocco. "He introduced himself as Ricardo, so that's what I called him."

Luca hummed but I ignored it and opened my safe, pulling

the gun case out to stash my pearl handled Glock 44. It had been a gift from my dad three years ago and the only gun I carried as an everyday piece.

After securing it, I grabbed two retractable serrated blades--gifted to me by Akira yesterday on Christmas--and my Glock 9.

"I'm ready," I announced while jogging down the stairs.

Ricardo was walking through the front door with my keys in hand at the same time.

He looked me up and down and said, "Moved your car into the garage."

I frowned.

"We don't need to ride together."

"Let me explain something to you..." He took steps forward and as bad as I wanted to retreat, I didn't. "When you're in my presence, you're in my care. I'm your personal bodyguard, chauffer, and whatever else I need to be when I need to be it, alright?"

"Okay," I agreed, much faster than I expected from myself.

It was the tone of voice, the seriousness mixed with finality.

Almost as if he dared me to challenge him on it.

Though his cool demeanor hadn't changed, he seemed hesitant about how quickly I'd given in. I didn't want to go on this trip with him but being difficult because of it wasn't on my agenda.

I wanted nothing more than for us to be cordial while we worked along aside one another.

"We good to go?" he asked, pulling us from that awkward moment.

"Yup, as soon as I grab my snacks for the flight..." I moved into the kitchen and opened the pantry. "Do you like sweets? I have some healthy stuff, too. Or--"

His breath on my neck stole the words from my mouth.

Why is he so close?

"I'll take a couple of those oatmeal creme pies."

He reached around me to dig into the already opened box.

"Thanks, Shortcake," he said, voice sing-song as he retreated and my lungs found air.

I took a moment to gather myself.

Shortcake?

I glanced at the two unopened boxes of my favorite snack and snatched them up, deciding to ignore the very cute nickname he'd suddenly given me.

It was a shame how easily impressed I could be at times.

"Got everything you need?" he asked as I reluctantly slipped into his car.

I nodded and opened one of my snack boxes, needing something to keep me occupied during the ride. The urge to climb into the back seat and stretch out was strong but I managed to stay seated as he pulled from the driveway.

"Where are we staying?" I asked, realizing I agreed with no real details on what would happen when we got to our destination.

This wasn't a job that required a safehouse.

"My place," he answered lazily, his words barely audible.

It annoyed me, not because he wasn't speaking louder and clearer but because I understood exactly what he said without needing him to repeat it.

"Your place?" I stuffed an empty wrapper in the snack box and cut my gaze at him. "In D.C.?"

His eyes met mine but only briefly.

"Yeah, it's where I'm from. I have a house."

Oh.

I turned away and stared out my window, mind in overdrive over such a small detail.

He had a house, a *home*.

"Do you have a house in Jersey?" I asked softly, too nosy not to.

"Nah, an apartment."

His tone had been airy, like a wave off and I let the conversation end there.

The silence for the rest of the ride hadn't been as uncomfortable as I expected and when we arrived at the airstrip, I didn't rush to get out like planned.

But as time moved and Ricardo hadn't either, I realized he was patiently waiting for me.

"You can--"

"I move when you do," he cut in.

With a sigh, I gathered my stuff and got out.

I had only wanted a second alone to breathe freely, before I spent six weeks dancing around this man in his *home* with no real privacy.

"This doesn't look like the Bianchi's jet," I murmured to myself, eyeing the unfamiliar maroon and black private plane.

"That's because it isn't."

His deep baritone rang closely to my ear and moved up my goddamn spine, giving me chills. The simple sound of his voice was enough to wake me up inside and I hated it.

Rocco moved toward the attendant standing at the bottom of the flight stairs, my bags rolling at his sides while his was slung over his shoulder. He allowed the man to take them one by one before giving me to space to walk up next.

Once inside, I moved down the aisle of the eight seater and found the perfect corner to burrow myself in for the next forty-five minutes--the shortest yet somehow longest flight of my life.

"You good?" Ricardo asked, his voice carrying through the

cabin as I placed my things in the seat across from where I decided to sit. "We can takeoff in ten."

I nodded and dropped down in my seat.

"I'm good," I said before settling my AirPod Max over my ears and silencing the world around me.

With my favorite LoFi music playing and eyes closed, I was able to relax for a short while. It hadn't been until I smelled Rocco's cologne that my body tensed again.

"Do you need to sit right here?" I asked, opening one eye to find that he'd moved my things and sat across from me.

I slipped my headphones off as his mouth began to move.

"For a brief second, yeah," he said, licking his full lips. "There's something you need to know before we land."

Intrigued, I lifted an eyebrow--a signal for him to continue--but he took his sweet time.

There were moments where I couldn't stare at him for too long, but other's--like now--where looking away wasn't an option. Maybe it was the stubborn woman inside me, who was raised by a monster that wouldn't allow it, or maybe it was something else entirely at play here.

I had no fucking clue and wished he'd speak to put me out of my misery.

"My family will be around," he finally said, eyeing me closely.

I wasn't sure if he was looking for a reaction or not and murmured, "Okay, cool," before looking away.

His family being around didn't exactly bother me, but it meant I had to be a little more cautious.

Great.

"Gaia," he drawled slowly, a flicker of emotion in his voice that had my gaze snapping to his again. "It ain't as simple as *okay cool.*"

I licked my lips but stopped as he'd began to follow the movement of my tongue.

"You're trying to tell me something. Lay it out there and I'll move accordingly."

Whatever was bothering him was beginning to bother me.

He brushed a hand down his face and stood.

The frustration emanating from him wasn't normal.

Ricardo didn't show frustration or any emotion for that matter, but right before my eyes and more than once, he'd given me a glimpse of a person I'd never met before.

"You'll have to see the shit for yourself to understand," he said, moving two rows up and choosing a seat that faced away from me. "I apologize in advance."

His warning filled me with curiosity.

Who the fuck is this man foreal?

CHAPTER 4
ROCCO

Gaia frustrated the fuck out of me in every way possible.

She was afraid of my presence, of the person I presented myself to be.

Even now, the nervous energy rolled off her in waves as I drove through D.C. toward my home. I'd never been more bothered by a person's view of who I am than with her.

"Ricardo," she called softly as the city disappeared and a thick brush of trees lined the highway in its wake. "How far out do you live?"

I slanted a look in her direction for a second, taking in her profile.

She sat with her body angled away from me but that didn't matter. It was her pretty as face that I cared about seeing freely. I wondered if she knew how fine she was.

"Another ten minutes," I replied after focusing on the road again.

We rode those minutes in silence and it wasn't until I

pulled into an enclosed tunnel that led into my underground garage that she spoke again.

"How many people do you live with?"

I frowned as I parked in the spot closest to the entrance, confused by her question.

"The cars," she elaborated, pointing. "There are six of them."

"Those belong to me..." I chuckled as her eyes pinched together into little slits. "Seems like a lot but it ain't. Most were gifts from other people."

She gave me her pretty eyes, the dark irises doing their best to figure me out.

"Won't be that easy," I mused, pushing my door open. "Come on. It's late now. I'll show you where you'll be sleeping and give you a tour tomorrow."

I grabbed our bags from the trunk and started toward the lower level entrance.

Though I couldn't see Gaia, I felt her trailing slowly behind me.

She was the nosy kind, more than likely eyeing every detail she could before trying to catch up. I entered the mudroom that would lead us into a smaller enclosed area with a flight of stairs and elevator.

"It smells good," she said softly, speaking more to herself than me.

It smelled like my younger sister and I almost turned us both around, not wanting to see her just yet. But Allyson wasn't the type to invade someone's space without letting them know first, which meant she'd been here but made sure to be gone before I would arrive.

Because I spent ninety percent of my time in New Jersey, my sisters and the staff I had on payroll kept my place spotless.

Ally knew I'd be in town and more than likely filled my fridge and cabinets.

"Oh, thank God there's an elevator. I hate stairs."

I smiled a little before turning to face her after we entered the enclosed space together.

"But you run four to six miles almost every day?"

Her gaze drifted in my direction as we began to ascend and I chuckled a little.

To her I sounded like a fucking stalker and maybe I was.

Gaia had a routine, that wasn't exactly safe, but she was heavily protected in Blackthorne. Living in the same community as Luca added on an extra layer that I appreciated.

"How do you know that?"

"Lucia mentioned it," I told her, not lying but also not telling the complete truth.

She hummed but didn't respond, which I was grateful for.

The elevator door opened on the second level, where Gaia would be staying.

My home was much larger than one man needed, but I'd had it built on the guise of having a family one day. Maybe even hosting family and friends on occasion, if needed.

The second level housed five bedroom suites and I rolled Gaia's suitcases toward the largest of them, stopping at the door and taking a step back to give her the space she'd need to enter.

"This is all you," I muttered, barely looking her in the eye as I started to retreat. "There's an intercom in every room, so if you need me hit the red button and I'll hear you."

I could feel her gaze on my back and turned to get a look at her over my shoulder.

"What's wrong?" I asked, noticing the distressed look on her face before she schooled it.

She looked down and shook her head.

"Nothing, sorry. I'll see you in the morning?"

I nodded, though I wished she would've spoke up about what was bothering her.

"Bright and early," I confirmed, turning but stopping myself once more. "Are you hungry?"

She bit her lip instead of responding and it agitated the fuck out of me.

I couldn't stop myself from striding into her personal space afterward.

"Ricardo..." Her back hit the door and I locked her in with my arms. "I--you..."

Our eyes danced, hers filled with something I couldn't place, and mine... I had no idea what they showed, but whatever it was didn't scare her this time around.

"Is it hard to speak in full sentences when I'm this close?" I asked, lips brushing the shell of her ear.

Her chest heaved against mine as I leaned in closer to get a whiff of her perfume. It was subtle, floral and something citrus, but fuck if it didn't make my dick hard.

She took small breaths and then stated calmly, "I'd really hate to get blood on your carpet."

Something sharp poked me through my shirt, not enough to draw blood but the warning was clear and I smirked, liking her feisty side.

"I know someone who's great at getting blood out of carpet. One phone call and it'll be like it never happened."

Gaia chuckled a little and I took that step back, understanding it more than she would know. Nothing I'd said amused her, if anything, it proved I was as unhinged as she'd guessed.

"Good night, Shortcake," I tossed out as I moved toward the elevator, this time continuing forward without stopping. "If you're hungry, the kitchen is on the first floor. Help yourself to whatever is there..." I stepped into the elevator and turned to find her standing in the same place I'd left her. "For the next six weeks, this is your home as much as it is mine. Take advantage."

The doors shut and I brushed a hand down my face, annoyed with myself for not sticking with the plan.

Give her space.

Show her the real me.

Never *ever* make her feel uncomfortable.

That woman... she'd fucked my head up and I wasn't sure what to do about it or myself for that matter.

I took the elevator down to the first floor, just to be sure Ally had brought food. After finding that I'd been right, I went up to the third floor with my single bag in tow.

Everything I needed, other than a kitchen was up on this level.

The master suite, a full bath, living area and an additional room that I'd turned into a workout and security room. Just off the living room was a large wraparound terrace that I spent a lot of time on; rain, snow, or sunshine.

I went straight for it after tossing my bag on the floor near the end of the sofa.

The glass door doubled as floor to ceiling windows and I slid it back, stepping into the chilly night. The weight on my shoulders lifted immediately and I reveled in the release.

Being home meant the mask could drop, at least until my family fucked up my good mood.

I loved D.C.

It was the only place I wanted to settle down in, and Enzo knew once I felt the urge to move on from the mafia I would. In the years I'd been working for his family, the feeling hadn't hit until I met her.

Gaia had been standing toe to toe with Brandon--Enzo and

Matteo's cousin--who managed the day-to-day operations of the casino in Grayfall. He was a control freak and from their encounter so was my feisty little hacker.

Eventually, they'd come to an agreement and squashed their feud.

The sound of the glass door sliding open below caught my attention, and I stepped closer to the railing to get a better look. As I peered over, I caught sight of Gaia's slender frame in a pair of loose fitting shorts and t-shirt, checking out the scenery.

She'd went down to the first floor and for whatever stupid reason, I liked that she hadn't decided to stay cooped up in her room until morning.

The pool was covered in preparation for the snow bound to cover it, but Christmas had come and gone with no sight of it leading into the New Year.

I kept to the shadows and watched her peek into the pool house before turning to look up.

Her gaze landed where I stood but after peering in the darkened area for a short moment, she shook her head and went back in the house.

Chuckling, I retreated and unpacked what little I brought.

After showering and tossing on a pair of sleep shorts, I laid across my bed for far longer than I wanted without closing my eyes. The thought of Gaia sharing my home with me wouldn't allow rest to come as easily as usual.

Fuck.

I sat up and grabbed my phone, deciding to check in with Enzo.

"I take it y'all made it without Gaia stabbing you," he said upon answering.

"Something like that," I replied with a smile, grateful he couldn't see the shit. "Everything good your way?"

He was silent for a moment and then Lucia's distinctive voice filled the line.

"Ricardo, why isn't my cousin answering her phone?"

"What's up with everyone calling me Ricardo?" I asked instead of responding to her question.

She laughed and I frowned, not finding shit funny.

"I'm sure you'll figure it out," she mused, laughter dancing between each syllable. "Anyway, tell Gaia to call me back or I'll hop on a flight and disturb her peac--"

"You aren't doing shit but healing," Enzo said from the background.

"And who's gonna stop--"

I hung up before she finished her retort.

Enzo wouldn't win that argument and I didn't care enough to have a front row seat.

Instead, I got up and hit the intercom near the bedroom door.

"Call your cousin before she shows up and disturbs your peace. Her words not mine."

I went back to bed, not waiting for a reply, mostly because I didn't expect one.

But it came shortly after I got comfortable.

"She loves Enzo too much to actually come here when she needs to be resting. Pretty sure I'm in the clear."

The urge to respond drew me to the intercom once more.

"You ignoring her on purpose?"

"Not in the mood for questions," she replied much quicker this time.

What kind of questions? I wanted to ask but chose not to.

"Understood..." My finger lingered as I debated what I wanted to say next. "Did you eat?"

"You had brown sugar pop tarts."

Gaia having a sweet tooth was an unexpected surprise.

"What about *actual* food, Shortcake?"

There was a lengthy amount of silence that made me believe our conversation was over.

As I started toward the bed again, she said, "Not hungry for real food. Maybe in the morning. Good night, Ricardo. *Sleep well.*"

She murmured the last part but it was the loudest.

Loud enough for me to feel it in my chest.

Loud enough to put me to sleep much faster than my previous attempt.

Fuck did that even mean?

CHAPTER 5

GAIA

He didn't have *just* a house; it was a goddamn multi-level mansion.

I wasn't a boujie bitch, nor was I green to living a life of luxury, but Ricardo having this place with no one living in it while he lived his life in Jersey didn't make sense.

Who would leave this beautifully crafted home sitting empty to live in gloomy ass Grayfall, New Jersey of all places?

I'd tipped toed around last night, peeking in rooms, the pantry for snacks, and backyard where the pool was. His home was no less than ten thousand square feet with floor to ceiling windows all around, a few doubling as sliding doors.

It was breathtaking, every inch of the open floor concept was... it was exactly how I'd want my forever home constructed.

"Morning, Shortcake," Ricardo greeted, startling me from my thoughts.

I looked up from my laptop screen as he sauntered in without a care in the world, chest bare and littered in tattoos.

They covered his torso and back but there wasn't a single piece on his arms or neck, like he'd specifically avoided those areas.

He was so beautiful to me.

The way he wore his crinkled locs on top of his head, his solid build, though he was somehow slender. Maybe from his height but he was only six foot two.

I followed the deep ridges in his back and arms, admiring how they folded into one another with his languid movements.

"Like what you see?" he asked, his back to me as he stood in front of the fancy coffee machine on the counter.

I rolled my eyes and murmured good morning before turning my attention to the files Lucia had sent over.

"There's nothing here," I said, scrolling the empty unsealed pages of Angelo's adoption. "Nothing but his birthdate and the city he was born in."

A plain blue coffee mug appeared next to my hand and I reached for it without thinking.

"Thank you."

I met is dark eyes over the rim as I sipped the hot concoction made exactly how I liked.

Sweet.

He knew too much about me without having asked me first, but him knowing my coffee preference was safe. I was there when he learned it, had even opened my mouth and given it to him.

"They were wiped," he droned near my ear after leaning in to look at the screen. "Whoever facilitated the adoption didn't want anyone digging years down the line."

I nodded, agreeing with him there.

"You think the Bianchi's got him illegally?" I asked, sitting back in the stool as I pondered that possibility. "I wouldn't put anything past a mafia boss doing whatever it takes to make his wife happy. Has anyone talked to Martina or is she off limits?"

Alessandro was dead but Martina was alive and well and probably held all the answers.

"Off limits," he said, turning to look at me.

His face was extremely close and as bad as I wanted to push him away, I couldn't.

"She doesn't know anything though," he added. "Whatever Alessandro did he kept close to the chest."

Slowly, he leaned away and I took a breath.

"Do I want to know how you know that?"

He smiled and for a second it reached his eyes, brightening them a bit.

My heart danced a little at the sight and I quickly looked away.

Don't you dare!

"I asked her..." He moved toward the fridge and opened the freezer. "And I believe her."

"So, she wasn't off limits then?"

Ricardo turned with a bag of frozen pineapples and strawberries in hand and set them on the counter next to a blender. He grabbed milk from the fridge and then went into the pantry next for a container of protein powder.

"Most things aren't off limits to me," he mused. "At least, not when I'm asked to do a job. I might keep most of it to myself, but I always get the job done."

His eyes met mine as he dumped a hefty amount of fruit into the blender, a scoop of protein, and almond milk.

Before starting it, he added, "When I want something, I give it my all."

I felt the conviction his statement all in my goddamn chest.

He wasn't talking about this job, that I was certain of.

Feeling overwhelmed with his presence, I wandered into

the family room just as I had last night and picked up the only visible picture in the entire place.

It was Rocco in a cap and gown with two women flanked at his sides wearing big smiles.

They looked exactly like him, right down to those deceptively dark soulless eyes.

"They were the only ones who showed up for me," Rocco said from somewhere behind me, making his presence known before invading my space once more.

His revelation pulled at my heartstrings, even with the nonchalance dancing loudly in his tone.

"Your parents didn't show?" I asked, sneaking a peek at him through my peripheral.

He was staring at the picture in my hand.

"Nah," he muttered before turning and leaving me alone with my thoughts.

The fuck was that about?

I placed the frame back after one last glance and returned to the kitchen where Rocco was downing his protein shake.

"What's on the agenda for today?" I asked, closing my laptop, ready to bolt.

"Free day..." He leaned into the counter and watched me. "I need to pay my respects to a few people before we start bustling around."

I nodded.

"Okay."

As I began to retreat, moving around the island to pass him, he stopped me by stepping in my line of sight.

"I'm having breakfast with my sisters at eleven," he revealed, wrapping a runaway loc around his bun. "Come with."

I pulled my laptop close to my chest and squeezed.

"Is that a request or..."

"I'm requesting your presence..." He tipped his head. "I would like for you to be there and meet them."

"Okay," I agreed. "Sure. I could eat."

He nodded but made no attempt to let me pass.

I hated the way he made me want to run for the hills but also into his arms.

How goddamn wishy washy was I going to be?

"You should go for that run you missed out on last night. We have time..." He looked at his watch. "It's still early."

"It's okay..." I dropped my gaze but only briefly. "I'll go for a night run, if possible."

He finally stepped aside and I wasted no time getting away from him and the feelings swirling in the pit of my stomach.

"Anything you want is possible, Shortcake," he said as the doors closed on the elevator.

I was an idiot.

How could I think doing this in the name of being a team player was smart?

I scolded myself for not taking Lucia up on her offer to work with Rocco from a far. But she'd known I would do anything for her and tricked me by offering another option.

Damn you, Luci.

Thinking of my cousin, I dialed her number after closing myself in the massive room Rocco had put me in. It was the biggest out of the five on this floor, with a bathroom that rivaled the en-suite at my townhome.

"She lives," Lucia droned upon answering, her attitude evident.

"If I were dead, you'd miss me," I quipped. "So, quit with the attitude and ask me all the questions you've been dying to."

A tiny gurgling noise brought a smile to my face.

Ugh.

I loved babies and wanted at least four whenever God saw fit to bless me with them and a husband.

"Hold on," she said, tone lighter. "This little monster is killing my damn nipples."

I chuckled.

She was on the brink of letting go breastfeeding altogether, but wanted to stick it out for as long as she could. It would take Enzo stepping in to get her to stop completely, but he was allowing Lucia to conclude that it wasn't for her all on her own.

We were stubborn women and neither had a problem admitting to it.

Because our mothers had successfully breastfed, she wanted the same experience.

"I'm back," she let me know as I sat on the floor in front of the wall that doubled as a full-length mirror. "For your information, I wasn't calling to ask questions..." there was a pause and then, "Okay, I was but not anything like you thought. Are you okay? I know this isn't what you wanted to do."

I took a minute to put her on speaker phone and started to unravel my hair, taking my time since I wasn't in a rush and had already showered and handled the necessities.

It gave me time to think about how I wanted to respond.

From her tone of voice, the carefulness I sensed, it was apparent she and Luca had talked.

My hesitation to let him know I was good was now both their problem, instead of my own like I preferred.

"It hasn't been a full day yet," I said, checking the curl pattern my plaits had created after loosening the first braid. "But, I'm okay, I promise."

She hummed and I rolled my eyes, knowing she was analyzing my response.

"Not sure I believe you or that any of what I'm sensing has

to do with Rocco at all, but I know you'll come to me when you're ready."

She was right, of course.

None of what I was feeling inside had to do with the man I was sharing a space with, but he had been the cherry on top to my internal dilemma.

"When the time is right," I said softly.

There was a moment of silence before she asked, "You know I love you, right?"

It made me smile because Luci had never been super affectionate, not in this way at least.

She was more of the kill your enemy to show she cared type, but Enzo had softened her up, and lately--after giving birth--telling us she loved us had become a new normal.

"I know you do, Luci. I love you, too."

"Okay. Just as long as you know that this life will never come between that or our relationship."

Stupid emotions, I thought as tears pricked the corner of my eyes.

I knew it to be true but my heart and mind were at war right now, and I couldn't decipher what was what anymore. It was breaking my heart.

"Why didn't you tell me about Ricardo's house?" I asked, moving the conversation to something less complicated. "This place is massive and he doesn't even live here full-time."

"His house?" Lucia questioned. "I didn't know anything about a house."

Taken aback by that revelation, I frowned.

"Really? It's beautiful and had to have been built in the last four years. Every inch is encased in large floor to ceilings windows and doors. He could fit the O'Sullivans in here perfectly."

"Enzo!" Lucia shouted.

I chuckled quietly, realizing that I might've started an argument.

They told one another everything and if he was privy to this and hadn't clued Lucia in, she would feel betrayed. Dramatic but still true.

"*Bellissima*," Enzo drawled, his deep voice carrying.

"Don't beautiful me until I know if you were aware that Rocco has a mansion in D.C."

"Why wouldn't I know?" he asked, probably smiling at the murderous look I knew she wore. "He's never there. Wasn't at the forefront of my mind until now."

An uncomfortable silence filled the line before three distinct kisses replaced it.

"Yuck..." I let my finger hover over the end button. "Love you, Luci. Got to go but I'll call you later."

I hung up before she could stop me and ask more questions.

With my shoulder length curls loose, I did a half up, half down style and slicked my edges with my favorite gel before tying a scarf over it for security while I dressed.

I didn't know anything about Ricardo's family, so the perfectionist in me wanted to be prepared for everything or possibly nothing at all.

Maybe his sisters were wholesome stafford wives with two point five kids and ranch style homes with *actual* white picket fences.

I chuckled to myself because it was such a ridiculous thought, especially after seeing that picture of them at Rocco's college graduation. That was damn near ten years ago and I knew firsthand how time could change a person.

Deciding on something that was a mix of edgy and chill, I stripped out of my lounge set and into the black long sleeved bodysuit, sheer black stockings that I ripped strategically, and a dark purple jean skirt that stopped mid-thigh.

I glanced at myself through the mirror and nodded before stepping into the chunky soled combat boots Violet had gotten me for Christmas. She was the leather jacket, cargo pant, combat boot kinda girl and I always loved her dark aesthetic.

I would complement her choice of boot every chance I got, and guess she figured I wanted a pair. And she'd been right.

The designer brand she gifted had to have set her back a couple thousand.

Not only did that make me feel loved, but the gift alone meant even with her quiet nature she noticed me for who I was.

I noticed her too.

Hopefully, she knew that.

Shaking thoughts of my friend group away, I slipped on the jewelry pieces I wore daily, tucking the heart pendant my father gifted me almost twenty years ago. Over time it had been upgraded but the tiny tracker embedded stayed the same.

This life was unpredictable and it put me at ease knowing my father could get to me without too much effort.

I checked the time and then concealed my gun and knife.

A few deep breaths and I was ready for the day.

Was I though?

The question played over and over in my mind as Ricardo drove us into downtown.

For almost eleven in the morning, it was bustling with people.

I didn't visit the nation's capital often, but there was always a lot going on when I did.

"What are your sisters' names?" I asked, stealing glances at Ricardo.

His locs were down and past his shoulders and blocking the side of his face.

What I could see was the outline of his lips; he licked them and I turned away, feeling like I'd been caught.

"Marie and Allyson. They'll tell you to call them Ree and Ally."

I nodded and rubbed my lips together, making sure the gloss hadn't dried up since putting it on less than ten minutes ago.

"Ree and Ally," I mumbled to myself, picturing which sister was which.

I didn't realize I'd been bouncing my leg until Rocco's large hand covered my knee and stopped it.

Goosebumps littered my skin from the brief touch.

Ugh.

Why was I so affected by this man?

"Are you nervous?" he asked as we rolled to a stop in front of a single standing building with people milling about outside.

"No," I lied, running my fingers over the spot where his hand had sat.

People didn't make me nervous, nor did I care about their opinions of me, but for whatever reason meeting his sisters filled me with anxiety.

I didn't quite understand why.

"You're lying," he surmised, nonchalantly. "Usually liars offend me but..."

Instead of finishing his statement, he whipped into a spot that opened up on the street and proceeded to get out.

Though he'd confused me like no other time before, I followed his lead as he bypassed the hostess without a word or acknowledging glance.

We moved through the packed restaurant toward the back

where the crowded tables lessened and the noise level followed.

Ricardo stopped in front of closed off space and stared at the sliding door.

His shoulders tensed suddenly, making me uncomfortable for him.

"Hey..." I reached out and touched his arm. "Are you okay?" I asked, as his dark eyes met mine.

"I'm sorry," he said, turning away to slide the door open.

"What for--"

"It's about time," a woman droned, her distaste evident.

"You said eleven. I'm here at eleven," Rocco stated dryly.

I stepped in behind him and then to his side to find three women instead of two.

My gaze drifted between them, easily picking his sisters out.

The older version of the two, with a sleek bob and designer power suit on had to be their mother. Both Marie and Allyson--though I still wasn't sure who was which--resembled the woman but only a little.

Ricardo's apology started to make sense but I refused to show how annoyed being tricked into meeting his mother made me. Instead, I plastered on the fakest smile possible while the conversation commenced between the four family members.

"You brought a guest," the sister with her hair pulled into a messy top knot pointed out. "I'm Allyson but please call me Ally."

The woman sitting before me had kind eyes, a huge contrast to that picture in Rocco's home. She had a piercing in her nose and tattoos that covered part of her hands.

"I'm Gaia," I said, ignoring the tension filling the room.

"It's nice to meet you, Ally..." I moved my gaze to her right. "You must be Marie."

Marie was the complete opposite of Allyson.

Her eyes were emotionless and she was stiff as a board. She and Rocco looked more alike now that I was up close and personal.

"I'm Ree," she said in lieu of a greeting. "Are you Italian?"

The way she looked me up and down after asking the question rubbed me the wrong way, but I smiled and shook my head.

"I'm not but my God mother named me and she married a man who is part Italian."

She looked away and I took that as the conversation being over.

Before I could greet his mother, Rocco maneuvered me toward the six person table.

He took the chair between his mother and where I'd sat and moved it to the head of the table, putting Allyson at his right and me at his left.

"Ma, this is Gaia," he said after a brief second of everyone sitting in silence. "Gaia, this is Deidre."

As his gaze met mine, the expression in his eyes compelled me to play it cool.

I turned to find his mother glancing suspiciously between the two of us.

"Mrs. Carter it's nice to meet you."

She nodded and focused her attention on Ricardo once more.

"Ricardo, must you slouch?" she asked.

Her criticism of him was unnecessary and cold.

She hadn't even greeted the man properly and I was upset about it.

But Rocco shrugged her complaint off and glanced at Allyson with a smile that lit up his entire face. My heart skipped a few beats at the sight before returning to its natural rhythm.

"Wassup, Ally cat," he greeted, nudging her head with two fingers. "Thanks for stocking my place."

She smiled brightly after slapping his hand away.

"Of course. It was quick and took me no time."

"If he lived here you wouldn't have to do that," Marie chimed in, her gaze on Rocco but much more relaxed. "Still not ready to come home?"

They stared at one another and the tension was palpable until it wasn't and both smiled, surprising me.

"Good to see you, too, Ree," he said, shaking his head.

"Yeah, sure..." She waved him off. "Tell me anything."

The lightheartedness didn't match the energy she'd given off before and it confused me.

"But not your mother," the matriarch beside me mused accusingly.

Their eyes met and just like with Marie, the tension disappeared after a moment of dreadful silence.

"You most of all," Rocco quipped with a smile that notably did not reach his eyes.

"Tell me anything," she tossed back, repeating Marie's words. "How was your flight in? I wish you would have let me send the Lear."

"And have Robert tracking my moves?" Rocco shook his head. "Nah, I'm good and my pockets are heavy enough to afford my own."

His mother stiffened at the mention of money but didn't respond.

Did she know what he did when away from them?

"How long are you in town for?" Allyson asked. "I hope I get to see you more than once."

I fixed my gaze on the menu while they talked back and forth.

My ears were perked up, taking in the conversations closely, until the server came back with our drinks and took our orders.

Diedre and Marie had gone with light meals, two fried eggs with toast and no meat.

Allyson had gotten the same but added a double side of bacon with hers.

I listened closely to Rocco's full order of pancakes, bacon, and spinach and feta omelet before deciding I wanted the same.

"I'll have the same as him but can I have cinnamon added into my pancake batter?"

The server nodded and took their exit after confirming everyone's order.

"You're so fit," Allyson said, eyes on me. "Tell me your secret to eating what you want and still looking this fine."

"I--"

"She's a runner," Rocco answered for me. "But even if she wasn't, it wouldn't matter."

I slanted a look in his direction, waiting for him to elaborate but it never came. His mother spoke next, taking my opportunity to speak away.

"Six weeks means you'll be able to attend your father's birthday gala in a few days."

"Don't ruin his mood with that," Allyson spoke, shaking her head. "He hasn't even had breakfast yet."

"You should at least think about it," Marie said, clearly on their mother's side. "It's been so long and dad will--"

"Mentioning your father as an incentive won't get you far," he told her, a slight edge in his voice. "I won't be attending this year. Leave it at that, alright?"

Marie nodded and the conversation shifted to something less significant.

I chose not to engage, finding that observing them was much more interesting.

Ricardo wasn't mafia rich, his privileged lifestyle had started at birth it seemed. Maybe later but my wealthy radar had burst upon entry, and now that I could take in their appearance and jewelry pieces, I knew I was right.

Allyson was wearing three Van Cleef bracelets that had five thousand dollar price tags.

Marie's Rolex was the same one my mother owned and had set my father back about forty thousand.

The diamond on their mother's ring finger had to be at least four carats.

The Carters might've been rolling in dough but everything else about them seemed *off,* and the more they interacted, the easier it became to piece the puzzle scattered inside my head together.

Ricardo wasn't alone in his aloofness.

Learning that made me sad for him as if my heart recognized the pain he was hiding from the world. None of what I was feeling had validity but deep down I knew it to be true.

I understood.

"Excuse me," I murmured, standing.

Rocco reached for my hand before I could move and I met his questioning gaze.

"Need to wash my hands," I told him, brushing my thumb against the inside of his palm to signal that I was okay.

Receiving the message, he released me and nodded.

"I'll come with," Marie offered, standing before I could deny the unwanted company.

My moment to breathe alone had been stolen from me, but

I managed to keep a cool head and neutral face as she led us to the bathroom not far from where we were seated.

The moment we entered she stepped in front of me in what felt like a threatening manner.

My fingers moved for my gun before I caught myself.

That was close.

"My brother is not a come up," she accused without knowing shit about me. "Whatever you being here is supposed--"

"It's in your best interest to take about three steps back minimum," I suggested coolly. "But, more is appreciated."

Had she done this to Lucia or Violet she'd be bleeding out by now.

I knew I presented myself as soft spoken and quiet, pliable even, but Marie understood much quicker than others that I was neither when provoked and took those steps back.

"Now, if you're concerned that I want your brother for his money that's noble but unfounded. Is there anything else you'd like to discuss or can I wash my hands now?"

She stepped aside with a tiny smirk on her face that had me lifting an eyebrow.

Our gazes met through the mirror as I lathered my hands.

"I knew if my brother brought you around you were a fighter," she said, moving to stand beside me.

"You were testing me."

"I was confirming that Rocco hadn't brought someone home who would run for the hills when she realized how fucked up we were."

Mmm.

"Testing me was pointless. Ricardo and I are work acquaintances, nothing more."

She laughed, shook water off her hands, and grabbed a few paper towels as I watched through the mirror.

"You don't know *Ricardo* very well," she informed me, her tone airy. "But if you're here it means he's hoping you're paying attention. Nothing is as it seems, especially with him."

I dried my hands and thought about what she said.

"What does your family do for a living?"

She frowned and tipped her head.

"He didn't tell you?"

"Tell me what exactly?"

Marie took a deep breath and chuckled.

"Fucking Rocco," she grumbled to herself before pinning those dark eyes she shared with her brother on me. "Here's a hint: The United States Attorney General."

She shook her head and left the bathroom, leaving me confused but intrigued.

"Who is the United States Attorney--*oh.*"

I grabbed my phone from my back pocket and typed in the high level government position to be sure my assumption was correct. When the name Robert Carter popped up with a picture of the man in question next to it, I had my answer.

Those soulless eyes.

Like father, like son.

I couldn't believe it.

The highest ranking law official in the country was the father to a gun toting mafia enforcer who had real bodies attached to his name.

Laughter spilled from my lips before I could stop it.

Fucking great.

CHAPTER 6
ROCCO

"Can you think about it?" my mother asked, her arm cradling mine as I walked her to the car idling in the front of the restaurant. "For me, Ricardo."

I sighed, feeling the pressure to give in weigh on me.

"I'll think about it but don't get your hopes up."

She smiled for the first time since I'd arrived and it was nice to see, even if she'd already mentally tossed my warning.

"That's all I'm asking for."

I nodded and opened the back door.

"It was good seeing you, Ma."

She turned to me and said, "You know sometimes I'm not sure if I believe you but today I do."

I shrugged.

"Sometimes I don't know if I'm going to get my mother or the wife of the attorney general. Before that it was every other position he held to get to this one."

"Your father--"

"Is not my concern. I saw the people I needed to see and I

won't leave town without seeing you at least one more time, that's a promise, but it's the only one I can offer."

Without any other choice but to agree, she nodded and got into the town car.

"Your friend Gaia seems nice," she said, not meaning a fucking word. "But, remember that eventually you have to--"

I shut the door on her, not wanting to hear anything else out of her mouth.

My mother never knew when to let shit rock and if I didn't shut her out, she'd drive me up a fucking wall until I gave in.

I watched until the driver turned the corner and disappeared from view before turning to my sisters and Gaia.

"Mr. Parque, I'd advise your client to be very careful what she posts on public platforms," Allyson said, walking away with her finger in the air. "Absolutely not. I will bury her and--"

She moved far enough down the block to block out the rest of what she was saying before Marie spoke.

"We've been working this case that is driving the office crazy."

"You both are lawyers?" Gaia asked, eyes bouncing from Marie to where Ally was standing.

"We like the term fixers, but both of us can practice law in six states."

Being the daughters of the attorney general and having law degrees wasn't easy. Working in the judicial sector was a conflict of interest in itself and limited where they could and couldn't be employed.

Having the last name Carter on your case could garner more media attention than either Ally or Marie wanted, becoming fixers opened more doors than both originally thought.

Gaia hummed.

"Olivia Pope style," she said with a smile.

Marie chuckled.

"Something like that, only neither of us are fucking the president."

Gaia's eyes met mine.

"And your father is only the attorney general, not a member of B6-13 or some other secret covert government agency that isn't fictional."

"Yup," Marie confirmed, though Gaia hadn't been talking to her. "Actually, if he were part of some covert agency we wouldn't know. I should go relieve Ally from her hell. This client needs a reality check."

Marie walked away and I stepped toward Gaia.

"My sister told you."

"She gave a hint and I followed the clue," she explained, tipping her head. "You weren't obligated to tell me anything, Ricardo."

"But you would've appreciated the insight," I concluded, understanding what she wasn't verbally stating.

"Yeah, I guess so..." She shrugged and focused her attention on Allyson and Marie. "You're a mystery to me. I thought... never mind. We should go."

I obliged and led us across the street to my truck.

As we settled, I made no move to drive.

"My father and I don't really see eye to eye," I said, breaking the silence. "We probably never will and while he's in office, I stay clear of his world."

She was smart enough to pick up on the tension his name brought to a conversation, but it was important she understood that every move I made wasn't to spite him but to stay true to who I decided to be.

"Does he know..." She looked over, her gaze softening as

our eyes met. "Does he know what you do while staying clear of his world?"

I chuckled.

"He pretends to know nothing, but he knows. They all do."

She nodded and glanced away.

"I... Thank you for telling me that," she murmured. "I'm sorry your relationship with your dad is strained."

Her apology hadn't been needed but I appreciated the fuck out of it.

Everyone around me had solid relationships with their fathers, for the most part. It magnified not having one with my own, so I felt that shit often.

"What about your father?" I asked, finding this to be the perfect time to get her talking.

I pulled from the parking spot and drove toward no particular destination.

"My dad..." She laughed a little. "He's the best."

"Yeah? Does he know what you do?"

I had to play it cool about knowing who her father was, and though it had been Akira who revealed his identity, I didn't want Gaia to think I researched her with ulterior motives in mind.

"Mmhm," she hummed, staring out her window. "I probably should've used my computer engineering degree in another way though."

There was something about how she said it that changed my next question.

"Don't like what you've been doing?"

She was quiet for a long while but eventually opened up like I'd hoped.

"I'm having mixed feelings about it all," she confessed, going silent afterward.

I drove us around the city, avoiding the turns and exits that would lead us back to my place. Gaia would disappear to the second level the moment we arrived and I wanted to be in her company for a little longer.

Even when quiet, her presence filled me up.

"Your sister attempted to defend your pockets," she revealed with a chuckle. "It was cute."

Fucking Marie.

"Appreciate you not harming her."

Marie was tough but she wasn't mafia tough.

"No need for that. I don't ever want to have to hurt a person but I will."

I believed her.

Maybe that's what she'd meant about having mixed feelings.

Deep down she was soft by nature, I knew it from the start.

"If you ever need to talk, I'm around."

I was close to driving us back to my place after planting the seed I needed to, when my phone rang and it resounded through the car speakers. Recognizing the unsaved number, I was tempted to ignore but decided against it at the last second.

"Yeah..."

The line was silent before Avery spoke.

"Your father is requesting a meeting," she said, getting straight to business. "It's non-negotiable."

My father's chief of staff Avery Montrose was a henchman in heels, never seeming to know her place or that I didn't answer to her and never would.

"I've never been the negotiating type."

"Good, tonight at--"

"Avery, tell my father to send his security back where they belong or I'll send them where they don't want to be," I cut in, watching the dark colored sedan trail two cars behind me. "When you're done, remind him of our agreement."

I ended the call and kept driving until my father's security merged and got off the highway. With my fingers gripping the steering wheel, I drove us back to my side of town with the intentions of dropping Gaia off and leaving to cool down.

"I need to make a run," I said, pulling into the garage and rolling to a stop in front of the entrance.

She looked over and I tried my best to avoid eye contact but she drew me in without having to say a word.

"You're upset," she surmised, frowning. "Maybe--"

"Gaia, I need you to go inside for me, alright?"

The words had come out much harsher than I'd meant but taking them back wouldn't change the expression she schooled quickly. If I had made any progress today, I surely fucked it up by not being able to control how my father affected me.

"Alright..." She nodded and touched her door handle. "Where's the track you set up for me to run at?"

"All the cars have the address programed under Port Field House. Take whichever one you want, the keys are in the box near the elevator."

She nodded and opened her door but before getting out glanced over her shoulder and said, "If you ever need to talk, I'll be around."

Her offer caught me off guard, but I couldn't react fast enough before she'd disappeared inside without a backward glance. As I contemplated taking her up on the offer, my phone rang.

The name flashing across the screen meant word of my arrival had spread.

Whenever I came into town and stayed more than a day, there were people who would want to lay eyes on me--Wyatt Barlowe being one of them.

If he was calling this soon it meant something good or *very* bad was happening.

"Meet me in Brentwood at the shop," he said, not giving me a chance to speak upon answering. "Got something I need your assistance with."

He hung up and I headed his way, pushing thoughts of confiding in Gaia into the back of my mind.

Brentwood sat on the Northeast side of town and was a hub for one crime syndicate, the Barlowe family. As of a year ago, Wyatt had taken his father's place as head of the family and I'd heard the transition hadn't been easy.

Though I didn't care to be summoned by anyone, not even Enzo, my interest was piqued. Wyatt and I had gotten into enough trouble growing up that I wouldn't be surprised if he wanted to relive our teenage years.

"Look who it is," a sultry voice droned as I exited my car and moved toward the barbershop's entrance.

My eyes zeroed in on a face I hadn't seen a long while.

If it were up to me, another twelve years could've passed before I ever laid eyes on Ophelia Brown again.

"Do I know you?" I questioned, staring into her big ass eyes like I didn't recognize her.

She still looked the same with her baby face, slightly chubby cheeks and baby doll eyes.

Ophelia had been the girl every teenage boy wanted back in the day and for a short while she'd been mine.

"Really, Rocco?" She frowned and placed her hands on her wide hips. "Stop joking around."

When the fuck had I ever been a jokester?

It had been silly shit like this that made me leave her behind.

She was good at playing stupid for attention and then using my name as a way to do shit I would never approve of had I known about it beforehand.

I pulled the shops door open without acknowledging her

disbelief and stepped aside, as a little boy no older than six came dashing out with her eyes and chubby cheeks.

"I'm ready," he said, game console in his hand. "Can we get ice cream before I go to daddy's house?"

Ignoring the glare coming from Ophelia, I stepped into the barbershop and was greeted by an old friend.

"Look at this chill ass muthafucka," Wyatt announced as he approached with his hand out.

We embraced for a brief second before I acknowledged the owner--his uncle--and the two barbers I didn't recognize, out of respect.

"Fuck you got me over here for?" I asked, turning my attention on Wyatt.

He tipped his head and led us toward the back, then down a flight of stairs.

"For the last two months," he started as we made it to the bottom where a large door made of reinforced steel blocked our way in. "I've been having an issue with my men being harassed by the cops. Product is being taken but no charges."

He turned to look at me as the door popped open upon code entry, his brows lifted.

"Either I have a mole or the cops have formed their own little criminal organization off my shit."

I hummed as we entered the security room, not exactly surprised but intrigued.

"And I can help you how?"

He chuckled and dropped in a rolling chair, sliding it across the floor to get to the screen at the back wall.

"I heard you were in town and brought someone with you, a hacker from the Moretti family."

I leaned against the wall and crossed my arms, using my silence as a response.

"She taking any side jobs?" he queried, swiping a finger

across the monitor to change the camera from inside the barbershop to the alley adjacent the building.

Wyatt learning who Gaia was before calling me had been strategic and while I didn't care for the display of power, I respected it.

"Don't know," I said, watching the silver truck pull into the alley on the monitor. "Probably should've asked her yourself."

He cut his eyes at me over his shoulder, squinting as if he were trying to figure something out.

"Tried that," he said, turning away just as the driver--his cousin Manny--exited and walked toward the trunk. "She left my server chat on read."

I chuckled.

Of course she had.

Gaia didn't work with anyone she didn't personally know or was recommended by someone she trusted. Most of her jobs, according to Lucia were for the family.

"Fuck is Manny doing?" I asked as he dragged an unconscious body from the trunk and tossed it over his shoulder.

"Bringing me answers..." He stood and opened a door that led down a hall and into another building. "Feel like having some fun?"

A door flew open and Manny dropped the man on the floor, startling him awake.

He flailed around, his voice muffled by a gag.

Manny had tied his legs and arms with rope, the knots in two half-hitches.

"Your knots improved," I spoke, earning Manny's deadly glare until he got a good look at me.

"Aw shit..." He covered his mouth with a fist. "Didn't know you were around."

I shrugged and walked toward the man who had stilled his

attempts to get loose; His eyes followed my movements closely.

"What kind of answers can he give?" I asked, kneeling on one leg.

His eyes moved rapidly as I watched him watch me, the fear emanating from him stinking up the gutted space.

"He was the first to get snatched up by the cops, but it wasn't until recently that this information came out," Wyatt explained. "I'm sure you get where this is going."

I nodded.

"Either he's working with them or he's working with them."

There wasn't another viable option.

His arrest didn't reach Wyatt because he more than likely agreed to something that got him set free and his product left intact.

"Start with his fingernails," I said, standing. "Take one for every minute he wants to play stupid. He'll talk before the second one comes off." I shook my head after watching him a little longer. "He'll talk before the first nail bed is fully lifted from the skin."

I stepped over him and toward the door, deciding to duck out through the alley.

"Not staying for the fun?" Manny asked, the sound of a body being dragged filling the air.

"Nah..." I glanced over my shoulder and sure enough he'd moved the man toward the anchors in the floor. "Not in the mood for blood getting on my fit. If you need anything other than my help getting to Gaia, I'll be around."

"Ayo," Wyatt called, following me into the alley. "How long you in town for?"

"A few weeks."

He nodded and moved toward me. "Must be important."

I leveled my gaze with his.

"Get it off your chest, Wy."

"I want a meeting with Enzo," he said, tipping his head.

"And I'm playing the middle man in this at what price?" I asked.

If Wyatt wanted to meet with Enzo he was looking to expand outside the DMV and doing so meant mixing my present and past.

"We were boys before this shit," he reminded me with a brow lifted. "I know the Bianchi's are plotting on moving into D.C., same as the Moretti's are slowly moving into New York."

"You want in before another family tries their luck?"

He nodded.

"Enzo is married to a Moretti. The connection gives me an in with Luca. That muthafucka refuses to meet because of his ties to Ace."

I nodded, understanding that Luca was loyal to those who were loyal to him.

Ace and Luca had history that hadn't started out good but ended with them forming a little alliance that didn't extend to the rest of the Delegation.

"Enzo is loyal to his wife and she's loyal to her brother," I told him. "Your only way in is to make good with the Callahan family first. If you can do that, I'll set up the meeting."

Wyatt hated what came with being in this business, but if you wanted to succeed you needed solid alliances. Sometimes that meant teaming up with people you didn't necessarily care for.

The Barlowe and Callahan families had bad blood that would take a while to sort out, but he'd get the job done, that much I knew.

"Be easy out here," I tossed over my shoulder as I moved down the alleyway with Wyatt's other dilemma on my mind.

If the Brentwood police were digging their heels into the drug game and succeeded even a little, it would spark a movement. Nothing ever stayed in the dark and there would only be a matter of time before word traveled up the coast.

Nothing good would come of that, not a fucking thing.

CHAPTER 7
GAIA

My workout fit clung to my sweaty body as I pushed myself through the last lap of my six mile run. The track didn't feel the same as running outside with the air beating me in the face, but it helped more than not being able to run at all.

I was frustrated and annoyed and I wanted to fucking fight.

That feeling wasn't foreign but I hated being consumed by my anger in this way.

As I came to a complete stop near my bag, I grabbed the insulated water bottle I'd taken from Rocco's cabinet and drank what was left inside.

Feeling a little of my anger dissipate, I picked up my towel and did my best to wipe the sweat from the exposed parts of my skin before leaving.

There hadn't been a soul in sight, only the guard at the front desk when I arrived. When I saw the donor name etched into a large appreciation placard near the entrance, I knew why I had the place to myself in the middle of the afternoon.

Rocco had funded the twenty-four hour recreation center

and continued to contribute every month toward their expenses.

"Come back soon," the young security guard at the desk called as I walked past it.

"I will," I said, smiling over my shoulder. "No need to shut the place down for me next time."

He grinned and shook his head.

"I only do as I'm told, Ms. Wilson."

I nodded and walked out into the chilly afternoon air, reveling in the way it cooled my heated body.

The sky was clear and bright and I had a feeling we might get our first snow storm of the season soon. With four days until the New Year, I was hoping for it.

I appreciated having a good sense of direction as I steered my way back to Rocco's in his fully loaded silver BMW X5. The seats were soft and it smelled exactly like its owner, almost as if he drove it often.

When I got back to his place, I headed straight for the shower and spent a long while standing under the spray while staring off into space. Eventually, I was able to pull myself from the trance and complete my shower routine.

Not long after, I was moisturized and dressed in a matching biker short set, long colorful knee socks with my hair gathered at the top of my head.

With my phone and laptop tucked under my arm, I stepped into the elevator and reached to press the number one but found myself hitting three instead.

Rocco had promised to show me the rest of his place but never got around to it.

And while I had given myself a self-guided tour the night we arrived, I didn't get to see the level he slept on and wanted to snoop before he found his way back.

The elevator doors opened into what looked like its own

separate apartment.

I moved into his private domain and spotted the pictures I'd been looking for lining the left wall. They were in black frames and included faces like Enzo and Matteo, his sisters and a few people I didn't recognize.

In the middle of the cluster was a family portrait, the only one with his father present. My gaze bounced from Rocco's face to the man he seemed to despise.

They wore the same bored expression as the rest of the family but I could tell the tension had been thick this day. Something about the way Ricardo stared into the camera spoke to my heart, summoning the lover girl living inside of me.

I wanted to hug the sadness away.

He was so goddamn sad.

"Didn't think I'd find you up here."

I jumped and turned, eyes wide at the sight of Ricardo stepping off the elevator.

"I was curious," I admitted, clutching my laptop and phone against my chest. "You have pictures up here."

He looked past me while nodding.

"I like to keep them close."

Slowly he brought his gaze to mine, a smirk forming along the way.

"You been in my bedroom?" he asked, ruining my chance to ask about the family picture.

I rolled my eyes and moved to push past him, only he didn't let me get far.

With his fingers wrapped around my wrist, he tugged me back and I collided with his body.

"Don't go," he murmured, staring down at me. "Were you about to work?"

The answer was on the tip of my tongue but I couldn't

speak, not with our hearts beating so closely together. I cleared my throat in an attempt to gather myself and he released me.

"I was going to reach out to a few contacts I have in the family planning field," I told him, able to speak now that we were apart. "It's probably a long shot but..."

I shrugged.

He nodded. "Gotta work all angles, I get it."

"Well, I'll go down--"

"Or you could stay and work in here," he suggested, cutting me off. "Bounce your thoughts off me..." He kicked off his boots and sat down. "Only if you want."

I bit my lip, not sure what I wanted to do but then my legs answered for me and I was sitting before I knew it. Once I settled my laptop against my thighs, I flipped it open.

"For the first time ever, I don't know what I'm looking for," I mumbled. "This just feels like..."

I shook my head.

"Something that shouldn't be touched," Rocco said, finishing my thought. "You could be right but it's not up to us."

"I know..." I peeked at him from under my lashes but quickly looked away after finding his eyes on me. "Hopefully no one gets hurt in the end. That's all I care about."

He hummed but I ignored the underlying message and opened a secured server.

<<kingjules3: Here>>

<m077y: Not a lot of time. What's up?>>

I uploaded the file to the server and pasted Angelo's birthdate.

<<kingjules3: Looking for birth parents or family.>>

<<mo77y: will see what I can find. Chat in twenty-four>>

I was about to close the server when a named I'd seen before popped up.

<<84r!0w3: You're the best, right?>>

I stared at the message, intrigued but annoyed.

Whoever Barlowe was had contacted me more than once, but this time he was bating me into replying and I was tempted to take him on.

<<84r!0w3: Ask the person you came into my city with about me.>>

I frowned and looked over at Rocco, who was staring at his phone.

For a while, I watched him, wondering if it was him who'd been messaging me. But as his fingers moved coolly across his phone's screen and nothing popped up in the server I concluded it wasn't him.

"You know someone connected to the name Barlowe?" I asked, gaining his undivided attention.

He stretched out before responding, crossing his legs at the ankle and rolling his head to the side to look at me.

"Wyatt Barlowe. Head of the Barlowe crime family."

Ah.

"He knows I'm here with you…"

Rocco nodded and looked up at the ceiling.

"Asked me to put in a good word so you'd work with him."

"But you refused?" I queried.

Though his face was slightly obscured, I caught the way his lips curled.

"Not my job to convince you of anything. If he reached out before and you didn't accept then that's what it is."

I glanced at my computer screen and began to type out a message.

<<kingjules3: I think we both know I am or else you wouldn't be here begging for my services.>>

I pulled up another screen and typed in Wyatt's name.

Modern day mafia men were more exposed to the world then back in the day.

They had businesses with their names attached to them, which left money and paper trails for me to follow. I loved when a breadcrumb turned into a loaf.

I hummed as his philanthropy work in and around the inner city populated on the screen.

"Do you trust him?" I asked Rocco as another message popped up in the server.

<<84r!0w3: I don't like to waste money.>>

"Trust is a term I use loosely these days but he's an old friend who hasn't crossed me in all the years we've known one another."

"So, you'd work with him?"

Rocco lifted up on his elbow and pinned those dark irises on me.

"I would if necessary," he drawled, licking his lips. "Don't worry. If he turns out to be anything other than what I believe him to be, I'll kill him slowly for you."

"You'd kill your childhood friend for me?"

I wasn't sure how to take that.

"For you..." He relaxed his body and tossed an arm over his eyes. "I'd decimate his bloodline."

My skin heated at the conviction in his tone, the declaration making me feel safe instead of turned off. I guess no matter how much I thought I didn't want to get lost in his darkness, there was no guarantee I wouldn't.

<<kingjules3: I take full payment up front, depending on the job. Break it down for me and don't leave anything out.>>

As if he'd drafted the message in hopes I'd want to know about it, the details populated in less than a minute. Once I familiarized myself with what he needed, I set my price, dropped the offshore account number and hit send.

He responded with a confirmation number three minutes later.

It would take a few days for the money to bounce around until it was untraceable and in my states account.

<<kingjules3: First update is in forty-eight hours>>

I shut my laptop and set it aside.

"Ricardo," I called, glancing in his direction.

He shifted a little but kept his eyes covered.

"Wassup, Shortcake?"

It took a second to work up the courage to ask, because suddenly I was nervous but my need to know took precedence.

"How are you feeling?"

He sat up and leaned forward, his gaze stormy.

"You want to know how I'm feeling?" he asked, almost as if he couldn't believe it.

I nodded and he leaned back, never taking his eyes off mine.

"If I answer that I'm not sure you'd understand."

He sounded so sure of that and I wanted to prove him wrong; I wanted to understand it. Most importantly, I wanted to understand him.

"Try me."

I pulled my legs up on the sofa and crossed them, deciding that I could wait all day for him to open up.

"My family doesn't believe it but I like being home," he confessed, lifting his socked feet onto the coffee table. "I want to be here but..."

He shrugged and rested his head back.

"Is it your dad that keeps you away?"

"Nah. Robert would rather I be around to control."

He never called the man dad, at least not aloud.

"Ricardo Carter can't be controlled, huh?" I jested, smiling to myself.

He chuckled and leaned forward but didn't refute my claim.

Our eyes met and I wondered what he was thinking about that had his brows pinched together.

"What?"

He shook his head and moved closer, leaving a small gap in the sectional between us.

"You're the reason everyone is calling me Ricardo," he accused, gaze dropping to my lips. "What's up with that?"

Did he not remember?

"You introduced yourself as Ricardo," I reminded him as he slowly closed what distance was left between us. "If it wasn't what you wanted to be called then..."

I angled my body to face his and uncrossed my legs, bringing them to my chest.

"*You* can call me whatever you want, Gaia."

I frowned and rested my chin against my knees, feeling comfortable in his presence like no other time before.

"Don't call me Gaia."

He rolled his head to face me with a brow lifted.

"What am I supposed to call you if not your name?"

"Shortcake," I murmured after burying my face in my arms.

How embarrassing did I have to be?

The truth was much simpler than I wanted to make it.

I liked the nickname and it felt right that he called me by it and not my government.

"Alright Shortcake it is," he agreed. "Now, do me a favor."

I lifted my head and he smiled.

"Appreciate you giving me what I wanted."

It took a moment for me to understand but the way my lips curled and then spread after getting it was such a Gaia thing to do.

"Ask me something," I requested. "Anything..."

"You didn't want to be here but came anyway, why's that?" he asked without pause.

"Because Luci asked me to and I'd do anything for her."

He chuckled but I wasn't sure if he found what I'd said funny or if he was disappointed.

"Do you want to know why I asked for you to be here with me?"

I was slightly taken aback by his question.

He had requested *me*.

"I didn't know it was you that wanted me here," I mumbled, chewing on my bottom lip.

"No offense, Shortcake..." He tugged on my chin, forcing my lip free. "I know you're good at what you do but I didn't necessarily need you here to help with this."

He traced the outline of my lips, while staring at me intently.

"Then, why am I here if not to help?"

As his fingers left my skin, I almost immediately missed the contact.

The gentleness I hadn't thought existed inside of him was there and I wanted to experience more of it.

"Didn't want to be alone," he admitted softly, his gaze leaving mine.

He didn't want to be alone.

"And you wanted to spend this time with me, doing what?"

Slowly, he brought his eyes to me again and the vulnerability dancing in them had the power to knock me off my feet had I been standing.

I reached out and smoothed his furrowed eyebrows, catching myself only after connecting with his soft skin.

"You can tell me," I coaxed, wanting to know the truth so I could move accordingly.

"What if there are no words to describe why I wanted you here?"

"Okay..." I nodded, still determined to know why, in one way or another. "Then, show me."

"I don't think you understand..." His fingers brushed the exposed skin of my thigh. "...how bad I want to fuck your world up right now, but it ain't that simple."

Didn't he know my world was already fucked up?

"Make it simple," I urged. "You wanted me here and I'm right in front of you."

I had no goddamn idea what I was asking for or why he was so reluctant to give it, but I couldn't bring myself to get up and walk away.

We had to see this moment through.

"Fuck it," he mumbled, leaning forward to... *kiss me?*

His lips brushed mine gently and then suddenly he pulled away without finishing the job.

I was on the verge of losing my shit inside, until he pulled his phone from his pocket and swiped the screen.

"What?" he groused, dragging a hand down his face.

He tipped his head toward the terrace door and went outside, leaving me alone and in my feelings.

My goodness.

Had I really been about to let him kiss me after only one day together?

Sadly, I was more disappointed than confused.

CHAPTER 8
ROCCO

"Have you thought about attending the gala?" Marie asked, her eyes on Gaia, who had set up her work station in the family room.

Her head bobbed to whatever was playing in her headphones as she typed at an insane speed. She'd been going at it since the wee hours.

We'd been tip toeing around one another for two days, her more than me, but it was probably for the best.

I didn't want her regretting a kiss, let alone one from me.

"Nah," I said, shaking my head. "I haven't thought about it at all."

"Rocco, you have to stop with this."

I looked away from Gaia and to my sister.

She had a mean mug aimed at me that wasn't as effective as it had been when we were kids.

Nothing about listening to my father thank a room full of people for kissing his ass all these years and donating loads of money to his causes appealed to me.

His birthday didn't mean shit to me either.

"Stop with what, Ree?" I asked, frowning. "The fuck are you even going for? Robert don't give a fuck about you either."

It was harsh but it was the fucking truth.

He'd become a *family man* for the image and nothing else.

"He's our dad," she stressed, trying her best to get through to me. "It's his birthday and you're finally in town. The gala is happening twenty minutes from here in three days. What's so hard about showing up for a short time and taking a few pics? Do you hate him that much?"

The guilt trips never got old and half the time they didn't make sense.

Marie hated our father; she cursed his name more times than not but for whatever reason she couldn't ever say no to him.

It was why I stayed away for longer than I liked. Being in the DMV was always a breath of fresh air until it wasn't. My sister wanted nothing more than for us to act like the perfect family when we were everything but that.

"Why do you love him so much? After everything he's—"

"Got it!" Gaia yelled, pumping her fist in the air.

She went back to typing furiously like it hadn't happened. Her presence made this conversation with my sister less annoying.

"What is she doing?" Ree asked. "She's like a feral computer geek."

I chuckled, grateful for the change of conversation.

"She is a computer geek and she's working."

"But what is she working on?"

I leveled my gaze with Ree's.

"Why?"

She threw her hands up and smiled.

"I'm only curious. You've never come home with anyone before and she's interesting."

"And when did she become interesting? Was it before or after you had words in the bathroom the other day?"

"Before," she replied, shrugging with a smile plastered on her face. "You didn't bring her here to work, Rocco. Is that why you won't attend the gala?"

I turned away from her and opened the fridge, looking for nothing in particular.

"Does she even know about—"

"Drop it, Ree," I snapped, tired of her questions. "You brought something for me, right?"

She jumped into action, sensing my mood. After grabbing a large Manila envelope from her bag, she slid it across the counter.

"I found this in an old file cabinet mom asked me to get rid of."

I peeked inside for a glimpse.

"Aunt Lina's will?"

My father's sister had passed almost six years ago from a drug overdose.

She didn't have children and she'd never been married.

To my knowledge, no one had ever actually gone through her belongings, which were in storage.

"When you're done being a hard ass, call me so we can talk about what's in there. None of it makes sense."

She stood and shouldered her laptop bag.

Upsetting her was the last thing I wanted to happen but the fucking Carter women didn't know when to stop pushing.

I fucking hated being pushed.

"Ree, I hope you know I love and would do anything for you, but—"

"I get it, alright..." She waved me off. "We just miss you and I know I'm not making you want to come home any time soon but I *really* wish you would."

I set the envelope down and moved around the counter before she could get too far.

"What aren't you telling me?"

She shook her head and pat my shoulder.

"It's nothing. I gotta go but I love you. Call me about those papers."

I had no choice but to let her go, even though doing so didn't sit right with me.

The fuck is going on?

"Hey," Gaia called, pulling me from my thoughts.

I turned to find her standing at the island with her laptop.

"Are you okay?" she asked, angling her head. "Your sister looked upset."

I shrugged off her concern.

"I'm good. What's up?"

She regarded me briefly and moved closer, sliding her computer in my direction until the screen was visible to the both of us.

"My contact was able to trace Angelo's adoption back to this place."

Legacy Adoption Services it read.

"Is this what your fist pump was about?"

She tossed a sheepish smile my way.

"No, that was about your friend Wyatt's situation," she explained. "He's got a big problem on his hands and it's not just a few corrupt police wanting his territory."

I lifted a brow.

"Not my place to elaborate but I'm sure he'd tell you..." She shrugged. "Anyway, this Legacy place keeps their files on a secured cloud that isn't really that secure and I was able to get in."

"You hacked the adoption agencies server?"

She had this triumphant smile on her face that I wanted to see more often.

"No, I hacked their cloud."

"The fuck is the difference?"

She rolled her eyes and pointed to the screen.

"You're getting off topic. Look at this!"

I eyed the pages she had populated on the screen, gliding my fingers across the mouse pad to zoom in on a few key sections.

Some of it was redacted, like the names of his parents and the hospital he'd been born in, but everything else was there.

"Is this what was supposed to be on those blank pages we were given?"

"Mmhm. I thought it was useless at first but I was able to find who accessed the files and when."

She cleared the screen and brought up a digital log book.

"It's the same name each time but it hasn't been touched in ten years."

Victoria Stokes.

"That name sounds familiar but I'm drawing a blank," I murmured to myself.

Stokes.

Stokes.

Stokes.

It would drive me crazy until I figured it out.

"I'm still digging but I'll know who she is soon."

Gaia reached to grab her laptop, more than likely to retreat to her work spot but I stopped her and closed the Acer.

"You need to eat."

"I had a—"

"If you tell me you had a pop tart or strawberry shortcake I'll lose my shit..." I pointed to the stool my sister had been occupying "Sit and I'll make you something."

"Ricardo—"

"You like to argue, huh?" I mused aloud, cutting off whatever rant she was gearing up for. "I prefer not to."

"Actually, I just hate being told what to do."

I smirked as she did exactly what I'd asked and took a seat, leaving her laptop where it was.

"I don't know..." I glanced over my shoulder. "Looks like you follow orders well enough."

"Whatever," she mumbled. "I'm just hungry, that's all."

I moved around the kitchen, deciding to make the only thing I knew how to cook without smoking us out.

"Are you allergic to anything?" I asked, pulling a red bell pepper, purple onion, and spinach from the fridge.

"Food, no. But I'm allergic to penicillin."

I nodded, storing that information.

"What about you?" she asked.

"Tomatoes."

"I'll keep that in mind..." She was silent for a second and then asked, "Hey, what's this?"

I looked up as she grabbed the Manila envelope Ree left.

"Not sure what it says but it's my aunts will."

"Oh, I'm sorry. I didn't know—"

I shook my head.

"It's cool. She passed five and a half years ago. Ree only found the will recently and said something about it wasn't right."

Gaia set it down but I could tell she was intrigued.

"Open it for me. Maybe you'll see what she does."

I busied myself making a quick veggie omelette.

Even though cooking wasn't exactly my forte, I could make a mean breakfast from time to time.

"This is thick," Gaia murmured as she carefully flipped through the stack of papers. "Wait..."

I turned from the stove at the sound of her voice, pushing the buttered pan back from the lit eye.

"That name..." she frowned. "It can't be a coincidence. They're too similar."

I rounded the island to get to her.

"What name?"

"Valarie Stokes..." She pointed to the small passage that mentioned her. "She was given one point five million from your aunt's estate as a token of her appreciation."

That didn't make sense.

"My aunt didn't have that kind of money. My grandparents left most of it to my father, aside from what was in the trust funds they'd set up for my sisters and me. They thought Lina was too irresponsible to handle the fortune properly."

"Really?" She flipped back a few pages. "But here, she left the remainder of her wealth to your father. With stocks and bonds, readily available cash in a few different accounts, it totaled about forty million."

She slanted her gaze in my direction and touched my arm.

"I think your sister was right. It doesn't makes sense if none of you knew your aunt had this money. Maybe your dad will know."

Of course.

It always pointed to him.

Shaking my head, I walked over to the stove and slid the pan back on the eye. I dropped the egg mixture inside next and watched it closely.

As the omelette began to cook, I thought about my next move.

My father had been up to no good my whole life, but this felt... *off.*

"Shortcake, how do you feel about attending a gala in three

days?" I asked, coming to a decision I hated having to make. "I feel like celebrating the New Year in style."

Gaia hummed.

"Sure," she said, agreeing much quicker than I expected. "I have the perfect dress."

I nodded but slipped my phone from my pocket to hit Ally up about her stylist.

After confirming that her contact was free to pull a few pieces to match the theme of the night, I plated Gaia's omelet and set it in front of her.

"Thank you, it smells amazing..." She took a few hefty bites and nodded. "Ricardo Carter, you make a mean omelet."

I chuckled and rested my elbows on the counter.

"It's the only thing I know how to make without burning some shit down."

She stuffed another bite into her mouth and then another before replying.

"I love to cook but I don't know how to make food for one..." She shrugged and cut her eyes at me. "Big dinners are thing in my family but you know that by now."

I nodded.

"Never seen your dad at a Sunday dinner."

Gaia regarded me closely, her gaze staring right into my goddamn soul.

She wasn't afraid to look into my eyes anymore and I saw that as progress.

"He's not the socializing for fun type," she explained. "And sometimes it's hard for two powerful men to share a room for too long, you know? He doesn't like change and dinners with the Moretti's keep growing."

I nodded and pushed myself into a standing position.

"That's what happen when people start to fall in love and have families of their own."

"Yeah..." She smiled. "I'm happy for them."

She longed for that, I felt it without needing to see or hear it.

"Don't worry," I mused more to myself than her as I moved away from the counter with her empty plate in hand. "You'll get to experience it one day soon."

Just keep letting me in.

CHAPTER 9
GAIA

New Year's Eve

"This is the first time we've missed bringing in the new year together," Lucia said, not sounding sad about it at all. "Times have changed."

"I'm sure Jaz and Violet are around."

She laughed.

"Jaz is spending her night with Dante and Violet..." She was quiet for a long second. "If I had to guess she'll be somewhere in O'Sullivan territory."

It wasn't news to any of us that Violet and Finnegan O'Sullivan had taken a liken to one another.

Finnegan had been obsessed with finding out who she was since before Enzo and Lucia got married. It had only been a matter of time before they found their way to one another.

Anyway," Luci went on, squinting into the camera. "Do you and Rocco have plans?"

I wanted so badly to look over at the man in question.

He was asleep on the other side of the sectional with an arm shielding his eyes.

For the last four days, we hadn't left his place and I didn't mind it one bit.

Everything I needed to handle could be done remotely and it seemed he liked to be secluded. It was something we both had in common; just two boring ass people who lived exciting lives at times.

"Plans?" I shrugged. "Not tonight. Tomorrow there's a gala for his father's birthday and—"

"He's going?"

She wore a deep frown that told me everyone had known his relationship with his father wasn't that great but me.

"Well—"

"Shortcake," Rocco called, his sleep filled voice giving me chills. "Tell Lucia you'll call her back."

I bit my lip and avoided looking into the camera, the urge to follow the command hitting hard.

"Luci, I'll call you back," I muttered, giving in to the desire.

"They can't know about why we're attending the gala," he said as I set my phone aside. "Not until we have all the answers."

He dropped his arm and patted the spot closest to him.

The sectional on the third level was L shaped and he laid stretched across the shortest part with his legs propped up on the arm of the couch.

"You want me to sit there or—"

"Lay here, head first," he instructed, watching for my reaction.

I moved my laptop and phone to the coffee table and stretched out, resting my chin against my hands.

"Wyatt invited us to bring in the New Year at his club tonight. I told him it would be up to you."

I frowned.

"Why do I have to take on that pressure?"

Rocco's lips curled into a sexy little smirk.

"If you say no I can blame you for being a recluse."

"But—"

"We ain't gotta do that shit though," he cut in, tone serious. "I'm throwing the option out there for you more than me. I know being away from your family isn't ideal."

I latched on to one of his locs and twirled it around my finger.

"It's no big deal. The girls and I were usually working some job into the new year anyway."

I thought about if I wanted to be out or not tonight and the possibility of seeing Rocco around people other than Enzo and Matteo appealed to me.

"I'm down to hang if you are," I told him, earning a sideways glance that made me smile.

"Yeah?"

I hitched a shoulder, playing it cool.

"Mmhm. I like to party from time to time."

"A Barlowe party isn't just any kind of party. They go into the wee hours of the morning and the liquor is free for the night."

"Sounds like a recipe for disaster."

He chuckled.

"You aren't wrong but we'll be gone before the shooting starts."

"Sounds a like a plan..." I yawned and adjusted my arms, laying my head in the crook of them. "In the meantime, I could use a nap."

"Not gonna lie, Shortcake," he murmured after a short silent spell. "I like having you in my home."

I smiled, half asleep already.

"Yeah, I like being here too."

It was peaceful and homey and the owner of this beautiful safe haven wasn't so bad either. He was... *special.*

And later that night, I was excited to be going out with him.

"Is this okay?" I asked, tugging at the hem of my long sleeved black mini dress. "There isn't a dress code, right?"

My feet were already killing me in my five inch heels, but I felt cute.

Ricardo—who had been standing near the elevator doors on the first level—turned as I stepped off. His gaze perused my frame twice before his eyes met mine.

Now that I'd found the courage to never break eye contact, I couldn't help but feel everything he was.

Those dark soulless eyes suddenly had a spark to them I wanted to explore.

"Turn around and let me see the back," he requested, twirling two fingers in a circular motion.

Dropping my head to hide my smile, I did a little spin and revealed the open back.

It exposed my tattoos, a slew of abstract art pieces I mostly kept hidden.

"A walking canvas," he murmured, the heat of his body close to mine.

His fingers stroked the length of my spine and I fought not to shiver.

"They mean the world to me," I confessed, turning to face him. "I don't show them off often."

"Why now?" he asked, closing the tiny gap between us.

"Because..." I focused on the pointed tips of my heels, feeling a little too vulnerable for eye contact. "You made me feel safe enough to be myself."

I looked up and he was on me, his large hands moving me backward until my back hit the cold elevator door.

He stared down at me with an intensity that made my legs quake.

Fucking heels.

I felt so goddamn unsteady.

"I hope the longer you're in my world, the safer you feel coming out of your shell."

"I... I hope so too."

He leaned in and pressed a gentle kiss to my forehead.

"Let's go," he murmured, hitting the call button on the elevator and pulling me into him as the door opened.

With our bodies pressed together, I took the opportunity to return the sentiment and kissed his cheek.

He smiled and released me without acknowledging the kiss, yet my heart still raced for him.

Ugh.

I was such a fucking sap and I wished I wasn't.

"Which one should we take?" he asked as we reached the garage level.

He flipped open the key box and glanced at me.

"The Maserati. Can never go wrong with red for the New Year. Plus, we're both in black and need a pop of color."

The Maserati Quattroporte was painted a cherry red with matte black rims.

"Who bought this one?" I asked as he hit the locks and the lights flashed.

"It was a gift from my grandfather before he passed a couple years back. I haven't drove it in a while."

"Oh..." I followed him around to the passenger side and slid in after he opened the door. "Hey..." I touched his hand before he could close me inside. "We can take another--"

"It's cool. I didn't give any stipulations before asking you which one."

He shut the door and I pulled my seatbelt on while watching him round the car.

"Did you two get along?" I asked, wanting to know more about his family.

"Yeah..." He pulled out of the garage and onto the street before speaking again. "He was a good guy even though he'd come from money, it never went to his head."

I nodded.

"What about your grandmother?"

He smiled and glanced at me briefly.

"She kept everybody in line," he mused wistfully. "But she was never mean. Her and my grandfather had an arranged marriage."

My eyes widened at the revelation.

"Arranged? You rarely hear about that in Black communities, wealthy or otherwise unless..."

Luci and Enzo had an arranged marriage but it had been their idea.

"The Carters are oil miners from Arizona and my grandmother's family—the Bensons—were coal miners from the same state. I guess they figured combining two powerhouses would solidify their places in the industry."

I rested my elbow on the middle console and placed my chin against my hand, intrigued by his family's history.

"Did it solidify their place?"

He nodded.

"But after falling in love, my grandfather turned down his right to the CEO position and it went to his brother."

"Wow. All in the name of love, that's so beautiful."

I didn't know his grandparents but I felt so happy for them.

That was the kind of love I wanted, where nothing could stop us from living in a state of peace and harmony. Not money nor power.

I hadn't realized I was so far in my head until Rocco called my name and announced we'd made it.

The outside of the club was lit up with an array of lights and movement from the people waiting to get inside.

"Do I need to leave my gun in here?" I asked, ready to remove it from my purse.

"Nah. The rules don't apply to us..." He opened his door and glanced over his shoulder. "Don't touch your door."

While he took his sweet time getting to me, I attached the chain-link strap to my clutch and shouldered it.

My door opened seconds later and I let Rocco help me out.

Once on steady ground, he shut the door and took my hand in his.

It was such an intimate move, just like the forehead kiss, and my heart danced a little.

The eyes of women and men alike waiting to get into the club followed our every move as we approached security.

"Oh, shit, you came," someone said as they stepped into the lighted area of the entrance.

He was tall and dark skinned with light brown eyes that had an evil glint to them.

But something about him gave off teddy bear vibes.

"I'm in the city, so I'm here," Rocco said, tugging me into his side as we bypassed security. "This is Gaia."

The man looked me over and nodded.

"I'm Manny," he revealed when Rocco didn't proceed with the introductions. "I see the real reason he decided to come celebrate the end of year with us."

I smiled and gripped Rocco's hand tighter.

"It was a mutual decision," I told him. "It's nice to meet you, Manny. Where are the drinks?"

We were standing in an enclosed space that sat between the front and club entrances.

I couldn't hear any music, which led me to believe that it was sound proofed.

"I like you already, Gaia," Manny complimented, pulling open the double doors and sending a rush of music through them.

He led us through the crowd until we came up on a flight of stairs near the end of the expansive bar. Before we began to ascend, a voice carried over the music and caught both Rocco's and my attention.

"Ricardo!" the woman yelled, using his government name this time.

We turned as she stepped through the crowd.

As her face came into a view, I admired her beauty. She was thick in all the right places and short, even without heels I knew I would stand over her.

Her skin was a beautiful Ebony shade and glowing from what had to be a shimmery oil or lotion.

She looked happy to see Rocco and I knew she was someone he'd fucked before.

It was written all over her face and body language until she looked at our hands.

I waited for Rocco to say something but he simply turned us around and led us up the steps.

"You're really going to pretend like we don't know one another for a second time," she accused from behind us. "That's fucked up."

A second time?

"I saw her outside of Wyatt's barbershop with her son," he explained before we made it to the top. "She's an ex."

I nodded.

"And you pretended not to know her?"

"An ex is an ex for a reason. I don't know her."

He was dead serious, leaving no room for debate.

I hadn't planned to argue with him about it because he wasn't mine, but I secretly liked that he acted as if she was no one to him.

And I guess in his eyes, she wasn't.

People had exes, some a little more delusional than others, but it was the way of the world.

I looked over my shoulder to see if she was standing at the bottom of the stairwell and sure enough there she was. Our eyes met and I smiled before turning away.

"This must be King Jules."

Because the man standing before Rocco and me was using my server name, I knew he was Wyatt Barlowe.

"Please, call me Gaia."

I pushed my freehand toward him to shake and Rocco reached out to gently push it down.

Wyatt smiled, showing off a set of straight white teeth that brightened his face.

He was handsome with a nice solid build like Rocco.

His eyes were the darkest I'd ever seen before and they held many stories, some a little too gruesome for even me.

"It's nice to meet you, Gaia..." He dipped slightly and pointed to the bar. "Drinks are on me tonight. Have whatever you'd like."

He and Rocco shared a look that I understood.

"I'll let you two talk," I murmured, grateful that the music on this level wasn't so loud that we couldn't speak in our inside voices.

"Aye..." Rocco griped my hand before I could slip it from his. "I'll be quick."

I nodded and stepped away from the old friends, finding me a seat at the bar that gave me a view of everything and everyone.

"What are you having, pretty," the bartender asked as I got comfortable.

Quickly, I scanned the wall of premium liquor.

"I'll take a finger of that Adcitivo."

"Finally someone with taste," she said before turning to make my drink.

I took that time to look around the room.

It was set up like a small lounge, enough space to fit about thirty people.

Feeling a set of eyes on me, I turned.

The woman sitting in a booth alone, didn't advert her gaze as our eyes met.

Instead, she lifted her glass and smirked.

Great, I thought.

Another ex.

Except this one was different.

She was confident and poised, showing off her obvious wealth.

This one came from his world.

"Here you are, pretty."

I thanked the bartender and picked up the glass, tipping it at the beauty in the corner before taking a sip with my eyes pinned on her from over the rim.

Two can play that game.

"She doesn't hold a candle to you, Shortcake," Rocco said as he slid into the stool beside me and ordered a drink.

"Who is she?"

He twisted my chair so that I was facing him and leaned in so close our noses touched.

"The daughter of my father's chief of staff."

I shook my head and leaned back, needing some air.

"Who is she *to you*?"

"The woman my parents wanted me to marry."

My skin heated at the revelation.

Jealousy.

It was an ugly trait to have but fuck if I wasn't feeling it ten times over.

"Why didn't you? She's beautiful."

He chuckled and picked up his drink.

"She's alright," he said with a shrug. "*You* are beautiful."

I nudged his shoulder.

"Don't try to sweet talk me, Ricardo."

Of course it worked and I was smiling like an idiot.

"There's no need to be jealous, Shortcake. I never wanted to be with her, never touched her—not even a hug."

I nodded, believing him.

"But your parents still want you to marry her, right?"

"My parents want a lot of things from me that I'll never give them, marrying Alice Montrose is one of those things."

I took another sip of my drink, letting all of this new information settle.

"Do you want to get married at all?"

"For love," he murmured, hand gripping my thigh. "It's the only thing that'll get me in a suit and tie."

He hadn't worn one to Enzo and Lucia's wedding now that I was thinking about it.

I smiled.

"I think you'd look handsome all gussied up."

He was about to respond when a hand landed on his shoulder and Alice stepped into view.

"I never thought I'd see you here," she said, her voice oozing with confidence. "It's been a long time, Ricardo."

"Not long enough," he replied, eyes on mine. "Alice, meet my fiancée, Gaia Wilson."

It took everything in me not to choke on the last of my drink.

Fiancée?

He was out of his damn mind and I kinda liked it.

Alice's eyes slid to my left hand and after noticing no ring, she smiled.

It was meant to be polite but all I saw was a smug bitch with an agenda.

"Oh, well, we should drink in celebration of your engagement."

She saddled up at the bar and ordered three shots of Hibiki.

I frowned at her choice of liquor.

Who the fuck took shots from a thousand dollar bottle of whiskey?

The bartender set three glasses in front of us and Alice reached for hers first.

"Let's toast to—"

Marrying for love and nothing else," Rocco said, cutting off whatever she'd been about to say.

"To marrying for love and nothing else," I repeated, tipping my shot down my throat.

It burned so good and I hummed in delight.

Alice chuckled a little and stood after emptying her shot glass.

"I'll leave you two *love birds* alone," she said, her eyes on me before moving to Rocco. "I hope to see you at the gala tomorrow, Ricardo."

"We'll be there," I answered for the both of us, my possessive nature rearing its ugly head.

Who was she to be calling him Ricardo?

Alice looked surprised and I wasn't sure if it was because we were actually attending or if it had to do with me being his guest.

Either way, it didn't matter.

She walked away without another word and this simple man laughed.

It was hearty and straight from the gut, bringing the dimples he hid so well out.

The person beside me was light and carefree, a far cry from who I was used to dealing with.

"You should laugh more often," I told him as I lowered my head to his shoulder.

The little bit of liquor I had mellowed me out just right. I could survive off this high all night.

"You like it?" he asked, caressing my thigh.

"Music to my ears, future husband."

His laughter vibrated through me and went straight to my pussy.

"How long before midnight?" I asked, regretting forgoing a watch.

We'd left his place a quarter to eleven.

"Forty-five minutes."

I nodded and lifted my head as the noise level picked up.

More people had filled the space and the party looked to have started from where we sat.

"King Jules!" Wyatt yelled as he ambled toward us with a bottle of gin in his hands. "Your drinks are free for life!"

I chuckled and nodded.

"I appreciate that."

"You know..." He leaned his hulky frame into the bar, a drunk grin on his face. "This is his first New Year's Eve here and I'm sure I have you to thank for that."

"Shut the fuck up," Rocco droned, earning a megawatt smile from his friend.

Wyatt looked between us and then glanced over his shoulder after Alice's laughter carried from where she sat.

She wasn't alone anymore, two women who I could only conclude were her friends, had joined her.

"I didn't know she was coming," he murmured, tapping the bar. "I wouldn't have let her up if—"

"It's all good. Gaia is good."

I nodded, agreeing with Rocco.

"She's harmless," I said, shrugging.

Wyatt straightened.

"Never underestimate a Montrose, Gaia."

He'd gone all serious, seemingly sobering up.

I smiled.

"I'm the one who shouldn't be underestimated."

He tipped his head as if trying to figure me out.

"Not just a famous hacker, huh?"

"Who is ever only one thing?" I quipped, earning a lazy smile from both him and Rocco.

"Don't worry about her," Rocco said, his confidence in me endearing. "She can handle herself."

The menace living inside of me wanted to prove Rocco's words as true and there was only one way to do that.

"Where's the bathroom?" I asked, adjusting my dress as I stood.

Wyatt waved to his left.

"Behind the curtains and down the hall to the right."

I nodded and placed a hand on Rocco's shoulder as I leaned into him.

My gaze purposely found Alice's over his shoulder, knowing she and her friends were watching my every move.

"I'll be quick," I murmured in his ear.

I went to walk away and he held me in place, his fingers digging gently into the exposed part of my back.

"You're up to no good," he said with his lips against my cheek. "No bodies or blood."

He released me and I walked past Alice's table, ignoring their stares.

Once I made it into the hall, I found the bathroom quickly and went over to the sink.

While checking my lipstick, the door opened and Alice walked in just as I'd expected she would.

What was up with women using the bathroom as a way to confront other women?

It was the worse place to corner a person, especially someone like me.

"There's something you should know," she said casually, stepping up to the counter.

I watched her through the mirror but didn't respond.

"He can't be engaged to you when he's engaged to me."

I chuckled and splashed a little water on a few wayward curls that had frizzed up.

"In what world will men not try their luck at having their cake and eating it too?" I asked, turning to face her.

She scoffed, her glossed lips curling into a frown.

"You're one of those types," she accused, taking a step forward. "The kind willing to let a man play them when the truth is clear. He was promised to me."

I shrugged, enjoying her frustration.

She was crazy beautiful and barely wearing any makeup.

There wasn't a blemish in sight but her soul was ugly and dark.

"Don't worry, Alice. When I'm done with him, I'll be sure to give him back."

I side stepped her and she grabbed my arm.

"You don't know who—"

"I know exactly who you are," I cut in, pulling my blade from inside my sleeve and pressing it to her exposed collarbone.

She gasped and tried backing away but the counter stopped her.

"But, here's the thing. You don't know who I am or what I'm capable of. This is your one and only warning, Ms. Montrose. Not only do I think it's best you never try to *check me* again over a man who barely looked you in your eyes but especially not over *my man*.

I released her and opened the bathroom door.

"I'm hoping you'll test my crazy though," I mused aloud before exiting.

When I pushed through the curtains, I tossed a smile at Alice's friends and made my way over to Rocco who was watching my every step.

"Did it make you feel better?" he asked, pulling me with enough force that my body collided with his.

I circled my arms around his neck, wanting to be closer.

"It made me feel..." I closed my eyes and took a deep breath, loving the way his cologne tickled my senses. "So damn good."

How had we gotten here so quickly?

Our eyes danced as Wyatt yelled it was almost time to countdown.

The bartender starting filling the shot glasses lining the bar for people to take but I didn't need any more liquor.

I was drunk off him, drunk off the way he looked at me like I meant something to him.

People bustled around us, grabbing drinks, but it was as if we were alone.

"I judged you all wrong," I whispered, cupping his face as the countdown began. "I'm sorry."

Ten.

Nine.

Eight.

"Don't be sorry," he said, guiding my face to his. "I hide myself well."

Five.

Four.

Three.

"You don't have to hide with me."

A slew of people yelling, *"Happy New Year"* resounded around us and I smiled.

"Happy New Year, Ricardo."

He kissed me and something inside of me woke, it was a part of myself I hadn't known existed. She was feral and needy, so goddamn needy.

"Happy New Year, Shortcake," Rocco said, his words muffled by my lips.

"I'm done for the night, take me home."

He pulled back a little and regarded me closely.

I wanted him so badly, my chest and pussy ached with need.

His true nature had opened my heart *and* my legs.

"Alright," he agreed, standing with me still pressed against his body. "Home it is."

Home.

It had a nice ring to it.

CHAPTER 10
ROCCO

I stood in the doorway leading out to the terrace, watching Gaia talk to her parents.

She was barefoot, walking back and forth with a little smile on her face.

"I'm okay, Dad," she said, shaking her head. "No, you don't have to come fuck shit up. I'm safe."

Something he said had her throwing her head back in laughter.

"I know you would. That's why I love you so much. Happy New Year to you too, old man."

She turned and leaned her back against the railing, her gaze finding mine and holding it.

"Hey, mommy," she spoke softly, a softer smile lifting the corners of her mouth. "Yes, I remember what you said..." She rolled her eyes but it wasn't out of irritation. "Anything I start, I can stop. I know. I love you, too. Happy New Year."

She pulled her phone from her ear and started to walked toward me.

"You turn into a whole new person when talking to them."

I pulled her into me and backed us into the house.

"I can't hide the real me from them," she said, dropping her phone on the sofa as I bypassed it to get to the bedroom.

"You are you," I corrected. "We all have different sides to us."

"If that's true then the same applies to you."

I nodded.

She had me there.

"That means I'm still the deranged man you saw me as..." I dropped my hands to her ass and turned us until her back faced the bed. "The one you were scared of."

She dropped her gaze and I lifted her head, never wanting her to be ashamed of her feelings.

"I wasn't afraid of you in that way," she murmured, her regret evident. "You just..."

She shook her head.

"What? Tell me what it was."

I needed to know.

Maybe I could change that shit or maybe this wasn't meant to be if I needed to change who I was to appeal to her more.

"I see the person I'm becoming when I look in your eyes sometimes," she confessed, pushing her fingers into her mane. "And I don't want to lose myself or who I am at the core."

"It's driving you crazy," I surmised, watching the stress cloud her pretty eyes. "Not knowing if this life is tainting your soul."

"It's..." She sat at the edge of the bed and I kneeled before her. "It is tainting me. Sometimes, I'm afraid of myself. What if one day I don't recognize the person looking back at me in the mirror?"

So, this is what she's conflicted about.

"Do you want out?"

She shook her head and then nodded.

"I—I don't know what I want."

"I know what you need…" I pushed my hands up her thighs, drawing her dress up until her black thong was exposed.

Her fingers found their way into my hair, the tips of her nails caressing my scalp just how I liked.

"What do I need, Ricardo?"

It took me a second to gather myself and reply to her question.

"You need me," I finally said, lifting my gaze to meet hers. "A safe place to unwind, to vent, to be your soft self away from the mafia. You need a man who sees both sides of you as enough. Gaia, I want to be your safe place."

I pushed her back and stood.

"You don't have to accept right away. I know there's still shit you need to know about me but I'm putting it out there that I want you. That cool?"

She nodded and slid back further before sitting up to remove her dress.

As she peeled the fabric from her skin, I admired what was being revealed to me.

Gaia was so damn sexy and it was hard to focus on anything but the way her body glistened under the dimmed lights. She was glowing but I'd grown accustomed to it.

"Rocco," she called, pulling me from my trance.

I pulled my shirt over my head and tossed it.

"Yeah?"

"Can you please fuck me? I really…" Her fingers danced down her toned abdomen and slipped into her lace thong. She tossed her head back and moaned. "…*really* need it."

Moving forward, I ripped the thin fabric from her body and pushed her hand away.

Her pussy was slick and calling out to me.

"Open up wider," I instructed, sliding two fingers between her pussy lips and sticking the wet digits in my mouth for a taste. "Mmm, you taste damn good, baby."

She writhed from my touch, barely keeping it together as I toyed with her clit until it peeked through its hideout for me.

"Please," she begged. "I want to feel your tongue."

I dragged her body to me until her pussy was face first with my mouth and went to work on my midnight snack, swiping and sucking on the supple flesh with vigor.

Gaia wasn't shy about what she wanted at all and I liked that shit, encouraging her to grab ahold of my head and feed me that pussy.

"Fuck," she cried, rolling her clit against the tip of my tongue as I slipped a finger and then another inside of her.

She lifted off the bed and I got up on my knees to follow, not wanting to let up.

I twisted my fingers and pressed them into her g-spot, smirking against her clit as she constricted around me from the contact.

Fuck, she was addicting.

I'd already been obsessed but the way she responded to my touch was enough to make me feel smug. Wanting this feeling to last, I released her right when she was about to come undone.

Slowly, I pressed light kisses up her stomach and around her breasts until our mouths were only mere inches from the other.

"Lick them clean for me," I commanded, brushing my lips against hers.

She obliged, cleaning the sticky essence from my mouth in two hungry swipes.

With her arms around my neck, she pulled my body close

to hers and murmured, "Put me out of my misery, Ricardo. I'm begging you, please."

Our lips collided and I refused to let up, removing my pants while keeping myself connected to her. She was everything I'd known she would be.

Soft and needy and feral for the dick.

Who was I to deny her the best sex she'd ever have?

I damn sure wasn't denying myself of her.

Almost losing the sense that God gave me, I reluctantly pulled away.

Gaia whined and I liked the sound coming from me.

I wanted her to want me just as bad as I wanted her to need me.

"We need a condom, hold on," I said, reaching to open the beside drawer. "Take your bra off."

I grabbed a few little gold packets, tossing the rest on the bed after sticking one in my mouth to hold.

When Gaia was fully exposed to me, I took my time taking it all in.

So, this is what was hiding underneath those clothes, I thought as she sat up and came face to face with my dick.

Smiling, she leaned forward and kissed the head, licking the precum from the tip.

Even though I wanted to feel the back of her throat, I wanted to be inside of her more.

"Later," I mumbled, sheathing myself and pushing her back.

She opened wide for me and I dove in, drawing back halfway after feeling how goddamn tight she was.

"Shit," she cursed, slipping her arms through mine and latching onto my back.

I worked myself inside of her until her pussy stretched to accommodate my girth.

"More," she begged, hooking her leg around my waist. "I want every inch, please."

Her begging was sending me over the fucking edge.

I couldn't control myself and began to thrust, fucking her with swift yet steady strokes that stirred me up and brought music from her lips.

Leaning forward, I got close enough to be serenaded, reveling in the way her moans caressed my entire being.

She was shaking beneath me, clawing at my skin gently, begging me to fuck her harder.

"I knew you'd be able to take this dick like a good girl," I murmured in her ear. "My good girl, right?"

"Yess," she whimpered back, her lips right up on my ear. "Don't stop. I can take it, I need it."

Fuck.

Her pussy gushed around me; I had no clue where I began or where she ended.

Was this what fucking someone you actually liked felt like?

I'd never experienced being so in sync with someone else's body before, let alone enjoyed it. Life hadn't afforded me the opportunity or maybe I was only supposed to have it with her.

I dropped my forehead against hers and slowed my strokes, pinning her arms over her head to give me more control.

"You got me," I confessed, probably confusing the fuck out of her. "Changed my whole fucking world just now."

I rolled my hips to dig in deeper, relishing in the way her pussy talked back to me.

"Oh my God," she cried, panting. "I-I... You're so fucking deep."

I sped up, fucking her into the mattress until her body twitched and convulsed beneath me. She gasped for air and I connected my mouth to hers, willing to give her every breath in my body even if it meant leaving none for myself.

Is this love?

The thought of loving and being loved by her made me cum so damn hard I saw stars.

Shit.

Gotta be love, I thought, falling asleep inside of my new home.

Later that morning, I woke to Gaia's body tangled with mine. Her hair was wild and in my face, fingers digging in my skin as she held on to me for what felt like dear life.

All while she slept peacefully.

At some point we'd cleaned up after our intense fucking session and fallen asleep again.

I brushed her hair back and chuckled at the way her mouth was half open.

She was so goddamn beautiful to me, everything about her.

The thickness of her eyebrows, those high ass cheekbones, her dark eyes... every fucking thing.

She had no idea that I saw her for who she was well before she allowed me to see glimpses. The parts of her she thought she was losing was there and called to me.

My phone rang and it snapped me out of my thoughts.

I grabbed it off the nightstand without moving, wanting her to sleep for a little while longer.

"What's up, Ally?"

"First, my shopper will be there in an hour," she let me know. "Next, did Gaia threaten Alice with a knife?"

I laughed.

"What the fuck, Ricardo? You know Alice doesn't know how to shut the fuck up. She's going around telling people that last night your side bitch—her words not mine—accosted her in the bathroom."

The more she revealed, the harder I laughed.

I hadn't asked Gaia what she did because it didn't fucking matter.

I was team Gaia no matter what.

Every action, word, and feeling she felt would become my own.

"Jesus, you're insane and apparently so is hat soft spoken girl. I should've known."

"Do you believe Alice?" I asked after collecting myself.

"Fuck Alice," Ally groused. "I know there's a little truth mixed in her story but most of it is more than likely exaggerated."

"She followed Gaia to the bathroom."

Allyson sighed.

"And all she got was a knife to the throat. I'm disappointed."

"I'm sure it was only a warning."

"Well—"

"It very much so was a warning," Gaia chimed in, her eyes still closed. "Next time I'll slice her pretty face."

"Atta girl," Ally said, chuckling. "Anyway, Mom is fuming. She said something about stopping by and that was twenty minutes ago. Sorry I'm just calling but I had a client issue."

"Working on the holiday, huh?"

"There's always a crisis to fix. I have to go but I'm glad to know you're attending the gala tonight. I'll finally have someone to talk about the guests with."

She hung up before I could respond.

"Is your mom coming over to scold me?" Gaia asked, opening her eyes with a smile on her face. "I don't think I've been reprimanded in a long time."

I chuckled.

"Nah, she'll wait until you aren't around and then talk shit. Typical Deidre."

"It's okay..." She sat up and stretched. "I'm not easily offended, besides I know how to win mothers over."

I lifted an eyebrow.

"How many mothers have you won over?"

She smirked and climbed her naked ass out of bed, throwing me off my game.

"A few. I used to be a heartbreaker."

"Mmm," I hummed, following her into the bathroom. "Should I be worried?"

Gaia turned and stepped into my personal space, her nipples brushing up against my chest.

"The only thing you should be worried about is me leaving bodies in my wake if another one of your exes tries to get your attention tonight."

Finding out that Gaia was possessive and had a jealous streak made my dick hard.

"Don't worry. I'll help you get rid of the bodies."

"I accept that..." She lifted up on her tip toes and kissed me. "Can't believe we're kissing now."

"Shortcake, I was all in those guts—"

"Shup up!" she yelled, covering her face. "I'm so embarrassed. We haven't been here long."

I let her wallow in her astonishment for a second before firmly gripping her face.

"Time don't mean shit. You were already mine, it just took a second for you to catch on."

"Am I yours?"

"What are you asking? Are you my girlfriend?"

She nodded and bit her lip.

"You're my fiancée."

Gaia laughed and pushed me away.

"Whatever. You were just using me to get Alice off your back."

"Fuck her. Be my fiancée now and my wife later."

She moved into the walk-in closet and snatched one of my shirts off the hanger.

As she slipped it over her body, I saw the contemplative expression in her eyes.

She wanted to say yes but she was afraid.

"You haven't met my dad," she said, brushing her fingers down her arm.

"Invite your parents here."

Her eyes widened.

"Really? You would be okay with that?"

I nodded.

"There's plenty of space and if me meeting your dad first is what you need then I'll do that."

Slowly, she closed the distance between us.

"That's really admirable if you. My dad means a lot to me and I value his opinion, but I don't think he'd actually come here right now."

It didn't matter if he came or not; she only needed to know that I'd be okay with it.

"Because of the problem in his territory?" I asked.

She looked up at me.

"How do you know about that?"

"Akira gave me a name as a way to win him over."

"What's the name?" she asked.

"It's been delivered to him."

"But you didn't want it to come from you?"

"I don't need an incentive to butter up the father of the woman I want to be with. He'd have to accept me eventually, with or without it."

"I don't know what to say."

"You don't have to say anything. Think about it and we'll revisit this conversation."

My phone chimed from the other room, signaling that someone had entered my garage.

"My mother is here, so I'm gonna head to the lower level. Come when you're ready."

I tipped her head back with two fingers.

"It doesn't matter if you're my girlfriend, fiancée, or wife. Just know that you're mine, alright?"

"O-okay."

I nodded and left her to go greet my mother, who was already inside when I made it down to the lower level.

"Please, tell me what Alice has been saying is a lie," she started the second she caught sight of me.

I didn't say anything.

"Ricardo, this is unacceptable..." She shook her head and set her bag on the island. "The Montrose family are a staple in our circle. Something like this—"

"The Montrose family means nothing to me. Gaia didn't go pick a fight with Alice..."

I caught myself before the laughter came.

What I was saying wasn't quite true but Alice took the bait and that wasn't my problem.

"It doesn't matter. Violence should never be the answer, ever."

"In my defense," Gaia began, making her presence known. "Alice put her hands on me without my permission. I felt threatened and reacted harshly. I'm not sorry for protecting myself but it was never my intention to cause issues in your circle."

She'd changed into a running fit that molded just right to her athletic physique.

"She touched you?" my mother asked, frowning.

Gaia nodded.

"Grabbed my wrist while I was trying to walk away from a

119

possible confrontation."

It was the truth, I could tell, but she was really selling it.

And I'll be damned if it wasn't working.

"I hope you don't give Ricardo too much flack about it. He didn't know until Allyson called, nor did he know that I would be accosted while using the bathroom."

The tension in my mother's shoulders lessened the more Gaia explained the situation.

"I understand," she said, glancing between Gaia and me.

"I'm gonna go for a run but I won't be long," Gaia said before turning away. "Only doing two miles."

She took off and when she was gone, I turned to my mother who was watching me closely.

"You love her, don't you?"

The question had been lingering in my mind since last night.

"I don't know but I do know that she's who I want to be with, not Alice."

She sighed. "I don't think I've ever seen you look at a woman like you do this one."

I stepped toward her.

"Look, I know you have this image to keep up, but I can't allow myself to be locked in a box for the sake of appearances. Nor can I fake love a person to make some other family happy. I need you to understand that I will never marry a woman picked for me, only the one I deem worthy enough to be my wife."

I pulled her into me before she could respond.

"I'm sorry I'm not the son you want me to be, but I would appreciate if you could accept me for who I am."

"You think you aren't the son I want?"

I took a step back, ready to avoid the question.

And thankfully the doorbell rang, giving me my out.

"That's the shopper with dress options for Gaia."

I went to let Norma in and guided her into the family room, so she could set up.

My mother eventually found her way there, while I looked over the pieces picked.

"I didn't know you decided to come."

I glanced at her over my shoulder.

"That's my bad, I've been busy and forgot to let you know."

"And you're bringing Gaia?"

I nodded.

"I need her there," I explained, feeling the need to do so.

For more reasons than one.

She nodded and stepped forward after greeting Norma.

"They're are beautiful," she murmured. "These shades of purple will look stunning on her skin."

I felt the same.

This year's theme was shades of purple to represent royalty.

"Well..." She hitched her purse on her shoulder. "I need to head back. My team will be arriving at the estate soon to assist me with getting ready."

I nodded and walked her to the elevator.

"Drive safe."

My mother had this look in her eyes that made me feel as though I'd hurt her feelings.

But, I couldn't take that on in order to make her feel better.

My truth was real and everyone needed to know where I stood on certain matters.

The doors shut and I took a breath.

"You don't have to wait around, Norma. I'll take them all."

She looked taken aback but I needed to fill Gaia's side of my his and hers closet.

There was no better start then a few designer gowns.

Once I got Norma squared away, I transferred the pieces up to my bedroom except one, choosing to hang the last option down in the room I didn't intend for her to use much longer.

Gaia would be the star of tonight's show.

PART TWO
"SOMETIMES VIOLENCE IS THE ONLY ANSWER."

- Ricardo Carter

CHAPTER II
GAIA

Never had I let a man dictate what I would and wouldn't wear, but when Ricardo mentioned he picked a dress for me I couldn't have imagined how beautiful it would be.

I stood in the mirror, not fully zipped, admiring the floor length gown with a velvet skirt and high neck transparent under bust with purple stripes. The sleeves were as long as the dress and flared out dramatically. It was beaded with pearls, silver stones, and purple jewels.

I'd decided on a triple bun look and stuck hair pins with pearls at the end throughout, to match the dress. My makeup was light but gave my skin a glow that made me feel as regal as the color meant.

Feeling beside myself with the choice, I walked over to the intercom and pressed the call button.

"Ricardo, I can't wear this. I'll stand out and—"

"You're supposed to stand out, Shortcake," he said, walking into my room dressed in a goddam suit with a purple tie and pocket square.

His shoes were black with a purple velvet trim that matched my dress.

"Wow," I murmured, stepping forward to fix one of his locs. "You look amazing."

He took my hand and brought it to his lips.

"You're always meant to standout, in every room you enter. Wear the dress."

Grateful that I hadn't applied my gloss and lip liner yet, I gnawed on my bottom lip.

"What kind of trouble do you plan on getting us into tonight?" I asked, releasing my lip and squinting at him.

"Us?"

"Of course..." I smiled and turned around. "Who else is going to have your back? Can you zip me?"

Instead of obliging, he wrapped his arms around my waist and kissed my neck.

"I want to give you something."

He zipped me and turned me to face him.

"What is—"

In his hand was a ring box flipped open and inside was the most beautiful ruby diamond I'd ever seen.

My heirloom radar went off and I shook my head.

"Ricardo..."

He took the ring from the box and slipped it on my finger before I could refuse it.

"This isn't about our conversation from earlier. Even though this ring can and will only belong to you, I wouldn't force an engagement on you."

I stared at my finger, feeling overwhelmed with emotion.

"I did tell Alice you were my fiancée and because she ran her mouth people will look for a ringless finger tonight and I can't have that. There will never be a reason for my father's circle of friends to doubt your place in my life."

He was so fucking thoughtful, how could I deny wearing it?

Truthfully, now that I'd seen the ring he planned to give to me if we were really to marry, I never wanted to take it off.

"It was my grandmothers," he explained. "She left it to me with the intention of me giving it to the woman I deem worthy of wearing it."

I clutched my hand to my chest.

"And I deem you worthy, Gaia Wilson. Will you wear it?"

I pushed him and he smiled.

"I can't believe you had those beautiful words inside of you all this time. Yes, I will wear it."

"Good..." He guided me to the bed and helped me sit. "Where are your shoes?"

I pointed behind me and he grabbed them, kneeling to put the purple velvet open toed Tom Ford shoes on my feet.

"Before we go, there's something you should know," he tossed out casually.

He pulled me up and fixed my sleeves.

"I'm listening."

"I don't trust my father at all," he said, tone serious. "Never. Ever. Let him get you alone."

I reached out and touched his shoulder.

"I'll try my best," I said. "But, don't forget that I can handle my own."

"I'm not worried about you..." He closed his eyes and took a breath. "I'm worried about what me killing my father would do to my mother."

"I'll be safe, I promise."

Rocco waited for me to line and gloss my lips and then we were on our way.

When we arrived to the birthday gala, luxury cars lined the streets and circular driveway.

The Carters had valet attendants outside but Rocco chose to park the black Escalade we'd driven in closest to the exit.

He walked around and helped me out, lacing our fingers once I was safely on solid ground.

"Is this your parents' home?"

It reminded me of the Moretti estate, grand in all ways.

"It's a venue space," he told me as we walked across the cobble stone. "The inside was stripped bare and redecorated. They mostly do weddings and parties with an occasional conference booked in the mix. My parents live in Maryland, not far from here."

I hummed and held on to his hand tighter as we came up on a grand staircase that led to the entrance. Murmurs of our presence was evident and I lifted my head a little higher to give them something else to talk about.

"Mr. Carter," the man at the door greeted, his deep voice shocking. "Glad to see you could make it this year..." His gaze met mine as he dipped his head in acknowledgment. "And you brought a date."

He held his hand out for me to shake and I placed my left palm against his.

"Gaia Wilson," I told him, giving him a firm shake.

"Ms. Wilson, it's a pleasure. Thomas McIntyre."

He went to release my hand and noticed the ring, his eyes widening at the sight of it.

"The rumors are true, I see."

I pulled my hand away and smiled.

"They are," Rocco confirmed. "I'm disappointed to hear that it was outed without my permission. Gaia and I had plans for a grand announcement but this will do."

Thomas looked between us with a sly smile on his face.

"Mmhm," he hummed, taking a step to the side to let us through. "Enjoy the night."

We stepped inside and was met with a sea of people in varying shades of purple.

"Thomas has worked for my family since I was a teen," Rocco informed me. "You can trust him."

I nodded.

"Ricardo! How lovely to see you," greeted a woman dressed in an off shoulder shimmery gown. "Your mother said you were attending and I almost didn't believe her."

"If my mother says I'm going to be somewhere, I'll be there," Rocco deadpanned, his gaze shifting to me briefly and then back to her.

Ah, we don't like this lady.

He pulled me away without introducing us and I laughed a little.

"What's up with her?" I asked, wanting all the tea.

"Her son is my half-brother."

I dug my heels into the floor to stop us.

"Excuse me?"

He pulled my frame flush against his and leaned forward, pressing his lips to my ear.

"My father is a serial cheater and she's one of his mistresses."

My heart ached for his mother.

How could she bare sharing her husband with another woman, let alone multiple?

"Does your mother know?"

He sighed and kissed my neck before pulling back.

"Deidre Carter is no fool."

Every detail I learned of his father made me hate him more and more.

"How is it that he can hide these things while—"

"Thank God, you two are here," Allyson said as she approached us with a drink in her hand.

129

She looked me up and down and nodded.

"Damn, girl. I see why my brother is smitten. Look at you."

Because I was easily embarrassed by the smallest things, her compliment made my skin heat. I wanted to hide but knew I couldn't.

"Thank you," I murmured, dropping my gaze to take her in.

She wore a blueish purple floor length gown with a split up to the thigh, a cowl neck, and thin straps.

"You look beautiful as well," I complimented.

Allyson did a little spin and pose.

"Thank you, I do what I can."

So confident.

I admired that trait.

"Did you see Yolanda?" she asked Rocco. "She's wearing the dress mom picked for herself three months ago. I wanted to claw her fucking eyes out."

"I saw her," Rocco replied. "Her boldness is because of your father."

"Yolanda should—"

"He's to blame," he cut in, tone clipped. "There's no reason other than he gave her the power to move how she does..." He looked at his sister. "Where's Marie?"

Allyson's gaze shifted suspiciously before she shrugged and took a sip of her drink.

"Is there something going on I need to know about?" he asked.

Allyson wouldn't respond, making it feel like something was amiss.

"Ally—"

"She's heading our way now."

I turned and there she was, wearing a gown similar to Allyson's but in a lilac shade with thicker straps that's draped off her arms.

As she approached, I couldn't stop thinking about how ethereal she looked.

There was a gracefulness to her that rivaled the stiff woman I'd met almost a week prior.

"I thought I'd have to man these people alone for a short time but I'm glad to see the three of you," she said, sharing air kisses with Allyson.

She moved to do the same with me and though I was shocked, I didn't miss a beat.

"I'm glad you decided to attend," Marie said, reaching out to swipe Rocco's wayward loc off his shoulder. "And you wore a suit. I must be dreaming."

"Couldn't embarrass my fiancée with my usual attire."

I glanced at him, surprised by the response.

He'd done it for me?

"Did you just say fiancée? We thought that was just a joke to get Alice off your back," Ally said, her eyes bouncing between us.

Rocco grabbed my left hand and as my sleeves fell his sisters gasped.

"Ricardo," they said at once.

But the shock was short lived as an older gentlemen approached and placed his hand on Marie's shoulder. She stiffened but made no attempt to remove it.

"We need to greet other guests," the man said, taking her hand without acknowledging the three of us.

"What does he mean by *we*?" Rocco questioned, removing his hand from mine.

Marie cleared her through.

"Pierson, this is my brother Ricardo. You two haven't had the pleasure of meeting yet. Rocco, this is Pierson Hugh. He's an associate of dad's and my fiancé."

Her revelation gave me chills.

This man had to be at least twenty years her senior. I wasn't a snob, love who you love, but Marie's reaction to his touch said something else was at play here.

"I apologize," Pierson said, holding his hand out. "I've only seen pictures of you."

Rocco stared at his hand but made no move to take.

"What the fuck is this?" he asked Marie instead. "Did Robert set this up?"

"Your father—"

"Aye, my man I'm not talking to you..." The base in his voice garnered looks from some of the people nearby. "My sister can speak for herself."

I noticed the way Pierson's hand tightened on her shoulder and she flinched.

Rocco took a step forward and I tugged on his hand to stop him.

Our eyes met and I knew he understood what I was trying to convey.

Not here.

"Dad introduced us, yes," Marie explained. "But marrying him was my decision."

Her eyes were pleading with Rocco to drop it or maybe she was begging her brother for help.

The urge to slice a few of her so-called fiancé's fingers off hit me like a fucking tidal wave. I *despised* men like him.

My entire adult life had been about sending them to the grave where they belonged.

The anger emanating off Rocco was hard to ignore or miss and I felt my own body rearing itself to attack.

I knew Pierson could feel it, his shifty eyes said so.

"I will talk to you three later in the night," Marie said, cutting through the tension.

They walked away and it took everything in me not to cause a scene.

"Rocco, you have to do something," Allyson blurted, forcing both our gazes in her direction. "Dad is... he's making her do it and I've tried everything to convince her otherwise but she won't listen."

I didn't know Marie well but she didn't seem like the type to take orders from anyone, let alone be forced into a marriage.

"What does he have on her?" I asked, going with my gut.

Allyson shook her head.

"Whatever it is she won't tell me. I just... I think he's hurting her and I can't bare it."

Tears clouded her eyes and she walked away.

"What do you what to do?" I asked, stepping in front of him. "Whatever it is, I'm game."

"You'll help me air this bitch out?" he asked, his eyes void of emotion. "I want to kill everybody in sight, that's what I want to do."

I nodded.

"Then let's air this bitch out," I agreed, ready to go to war with him and for him.

His gaze never left mine and I wondered if he didn't believe me, but I never got to ask.

The lights dimmed and Rocco turned me around.

"The guest of honor has arrived," someone spoke through a microphone. "Please, welcome, Robert Cater and his wife Deidre Carter."

As his father and mother entered, Rocco wrapped his arms around me from behind.

I brought my hands up and pressed them against his in support.

Deep down, I knew there were too many important people

here for us to massacre the lot of them but I would do it for him if he really wanted.

We stayed rooted in place as his parents made their rounds.

The closer they got to us, the tenser Rocco became.

I stroked his fingers, grateful for the dramatic sleeves on my dress covering our hands.

When his father stepped toward us, his eyes landed on me first.

He scrutinized me from head to toe, his expression never changing or revealing what he was feeling.

"Son," he finally said, looking over my head. "It's been a while. I'm glad you could make it."

Rocco released and moved around me.

I wasn't sure what he would do next but I hadn't expected him to play it cool.

"My schedule opened up and allowed me to make it this year," he said, holding his hand out. "Happy Birthday."

They shook hands and it was the most impersonal greeting between father and son.

"And who's your guest," Robert asked, returning his deceptively dark eyes to me.

"This is Gaia Wilson, my fiancée."

Rocco reached for me and I placed my hand in his, allowing him to pull me forward.

His mother gasped softly as I held out my left hand for Robert to shake.

"It's an honor to meet you, Mr. Carter," I droned. "Ricardo has told me a lot about you."

Enough to make me hate your fucking guts.

He took my hand but I pulled it from his after a second or two.

"I hope all good things," he mused with a dark smile.

I forced a grin but refused to respond.

"Mrs. Carter, you look stunning," I complimented, turning away from her bitch ass husband. "I hadn't expected anything less."

She looked taken aback but recovered quickly.

"Flattery will get you far, Ms. Wilson," she said, taking my hand.

Her thumb brushed over the ring and it felt like she'd done it on purpose. Almost as if she couldn't believe I was wearing it.

"We need to greet Senator Logan and his wife," Robert said, ready to move on.

I perched myself closer to Rocco's side as they started to move past us.

"We'll talk soon," Robert muttered for only us to hear. "There's much to discuss."

Rocco started to pull me through the sea of people, his long strides making it hard for me to keep up.

Eventually, he slowed as we came upon an empty hallway.

"In here," he said, dragging me inside the first room we came upon.

"What—"

He pushed me against the shut door and murmured, "I need a moment alone with just you."

He was angry and rightfully so.

"I'm here," I whispered back, enclosing my arms around his waist.

And I had no plans of going anywhere.

CHAPTER 12
ROCCO

"Mr. Carter, your father has requested your presence in the greenhouse," Avery Montrose spoke from behind Gaia.

She avoided making eye contact with her as Gaia turned to get a look at who was speaking.

"Avery Montrose this is my fiancée Gaia Wilson."

"Please, be quick," she went on, ignoring the introduction. "The charity ceremony starts soon and it's important to stay on schedule."

Gaia tipped her head and smiled.

"How's your daughter, Mrs. Montrose? I don't think I've seen her in attendance tonight."

We'd both seen Alice and her group of friends after I stole Gaia away for a moment to breathe alone.

If I allowed my anger to lead me tonight, my father would win and I couldn't chance fucking up why Gaia and I had come in the first place.

But seeing my sister in distress wouldn't fly either.

"You can leave Avery, I'll find my father."

She eyed Gaia with disdain but knew better than to speak her feelings aloud, not while I was standing here at least.

"I'm getting tired of everyone looking at me like I'm the enemy," Gaia said, her lips curled into a smile that said otherwise. "Go meet with your father. I'll be right here when you get back."

I eyed her skeptically, getting the feeling she wasn't being truthful about staying in one place.

"Don't get into any trouble while I'm away."

She waved me off and I grabbed her hand, bringing it to my lips.

"I mean it, Shortcake. Remember what I said before we left Blackthorne?"

She rolled her eyes.

"Something about being my chauffeur and bodyguard. Blah Blah. I'll be good, promise."

I glanced around for my sisters and spotted Ally looking in our direction.

With a quick head tip, I beckoned her and walked away.

She would keep Gaia busy.

I walked into the greenhouse where my father was already waiting.

"Robert," I greeted, leaning against the door. "What can I do for you?"

The eyes I'd learn to mirror growing up in order to avoid being chastised met mine dead on.

"Why is it that every time you come to town you cause a ruckus that disturbs my peaceful world?"

"And what ruckus might that be?"

"Let's start with you announcing an engagement without speaking to me first."

"I stopped answering to you a long time ago. Next problem."

He chuckled and took a step forward but paused his strides after I lifted an eyebrow.

It was a warning he could read well.

"Why was Alice threatened with a knife?"

"Why did Alice touch my future wife?" I tossed back, tipping my head. "We both know that brash behavior is met with consequences. Alice challenged Gaia and my girl handled it accordingly."

He hummed.

"Where did this *Gaia* come from?"

"Let me ask you something..." I stepped toward him. "Did aunt Lina have a will?"

"She did not," he replied without pause.

He was a good fucking liar.

If I hadn't seen the will myself, I wouldn't have thought twice about his answer.

"Who is Valarie Stokes?"

He shifted a little upon hearing it.

"Never heard the name before."

I nodded, playing it cool.

"Maybe I can assist with whatever it is you need answers to," he offered.

"In return for what?"

We were toe to toe now, both playing the long game.

"Marry Alice like I planned for you and move back to D.C. You and your sisters need to be with people who are on your level. You are a reflection of me, don't forget that."

I laughed in his face, appreciating the anger it sparked in his eyes.

"I'm marrying Gaia..." I shrugged. "But maybe I'll come home, only if she agrees."

"Alice comes from a powerful family—"

"Alice is a weak puppet. Her family are nothing but peasants with money and a little status. If you weren't fucking her mother—"

He grabbed me by the lapels of my suit coat and stilled as the tip of my gun touched his chin.

"Should I remind you that your position won't stop me from putting a bullet in your skull?"

The teenage boy he'd beat every chance he got was no more.

I wanted a reason to end his life.

"I'm your father."

"You're my sperm donor, nothing more than that."

He laughed it off and released me.

"You've always been sensitive," he accused with a smirk. "I see that hasn't changed."

His insults didn't faze me anymore.

To him showing any kind of emotion meant you were weak.

It took a long time for me to figure out that he was wrong and in the midst of that I learned to protect myself by wearing a mask of indifference.

"And you've always been a bitch," I deadpanned, watching him pause his strides to the door. "I'm grateful I didn't inherit that trait."

He stared ahead in silence for a long while and then said, "I expect you and your *fiancée* to attend your sister's wedding."

He left before I could respond but it didn't matter.

Pierson Hugh wouldn't see daylight.

I waited a few minutes before leaving, only to be accosted by Alice.

Snow had started to fall for the first time since fall turned to winter.

"You gave your thug a ring?" she questioned as if she had the power to do so.

Alice flipped her dress back and stepped closer.

"I always thought you come around, Ricardo. We could be good together. A power couple."

I hated delusional women who couldn't take no for an answer.

"Five years ago, what did I say to you?"

Her eyes bucked and she looked away.

"You wouldn't marry me," she mumbled.

"Say it louder so you can hear yourself, Alice. I won't ever marry you. Not then, not now, and never in the future. You can't tell me you've spent the last five years with your legs closed."

She gasped and stumbled back a little.

"Don't be crass, Ricardo."

"Then stop being stupid..." I walked around her while adding, "My thug is waiting for a reason to slice you up. I suggest moving on before I let her loose on you."

Marie was standing at the side entrance when I got there, rubbing her arm.

She seemed to be in her own world and didn't notice until I grabbed her.

I waited until Alice slipped past us and back into the party to speak about the dark finger prints around her wrist.

"Did he do this to you?" I asked, keeping my tone as calm as possible.

She looked away.

"Marie, why didn't you tell me sooner?"

"I tried but I didn't want to force you home because of my shit."

She'd been crying for help all this time and I missed the signs.

I grabbed her face, frustrated with her, but feeling her pain.

"Don't you know I'll paint the city red for you?"

Her eyes filled with tears and I felt my chest tighten.

This was my big sister, my protector in more ways than one and here she was still trying to protect me.

"I don't want you getting into trouble for me," she whispered. "He can't just go missing."

"He can go wherever I decide to send him."

"I miss you so much, Rocco. Can you please come home?"

"The plan has always been to come home eventually. I need you to do me a favor."

"Anything."

"Help convince Gaia to come with me."

"You really care about her, huh?"

I nodded.

"I really fucking do. She's not used to such a discord between family. Enzo's wife is her cousin and their family dynamic is nothing like ours. They're close as close can be."

"She's fierce but also kinda soft. I guess you can only be those two things with a family who cares for you."

I hated how sad my sister was.

"Don't worry, you won't have to marry him or any other man you didn't choose for yourself. I'll take care of it."

She shook her head.

"You can't—"

"I can and I will..." I took her hand and led us back into the party. "Let's find Gaia before she taints Ally."

Marie scoffed.

"Your sister is feral all on her own. She doesn't need anyone to taint her."

I searched through the moving crowd but didn't find them after a few pass overs.

"Do you see them?"

Marie stepped beside me and shook her head.

"No. Maybe they went to the bathroom."

I looked around again and shook my head.

Something was off.

"Follow me."

I went to the place I'd taken Gaia before and could hear hushed voices from behind the closed door. As I pushed inside, there was Gaia with her gun pointed at Avery's head.

Allyson was standing across from them, eyes wide.

"Shortcake," I called softly, shutting the door behind me.

"I don't like being threatened," she said, her voice deeper than usual. "But threatening my family, that's a big no no."

I moved forward and touched the back of her neck.

"How was your family threatened?"

"She um..." Allyson cleared her throat. "Avery said she would cause trouble for Carter and Associates if we didn't get in line with dad's plans to marry us off. Gaia overheard and came in and..."

She was protecting *my* family.

"Is this who you've decided to marry over my daughter?" Avery said, no real base in her voice. "This is absurd, Ricardo. Your father is the goddamn attorney general and you run with criminals. Where's the respect?"

"Respect is earned," Gaia sneered. "And who the fuck are you calling a criminal? *Me* or *him*? Last I checked criminals had records to show for their crimes."

She advanced on Avery and I was right there to catch and pull her back.

"Leave, Avery," I ordered. "And if you mention this to my father, I won't hesitate to expose your affair. We both know neither of you want that."

She rushed out and Allyson came running, throwing herself at Gaia.

"You're the best," she said, pulling my woman away from me.

142

"I have to admit that was pretty badass," Marie mused.

Allyson released Gaia, who turned to me with a frown on her face.

"Why did you stop me?"

"Because we can't clean up a bloody mess efficiently with all those people out there."

She bunched the bottom of her dress and returned the gun to its holster.

"Fucking uppity ass people. They're corrupt as corrupt can be and the world is supposed to depend on them to make it safe? Fuck that. I'll handle it my way."

She was mumbling to herself, not looking for a response.

Her words made me feel like she wouldn't dare move here to be with me.

I wasn't sure how to feel about that.

"Ricardo, I'm ready to go..." She looked up at me, her eyes ablaze. "I need air and real food and I want to cuddle my anger away."

I wanted nothing more than to bend her over right here but with my sisters watching us interact, I couldn't do it.

"We can leave," I agreed, turning to look at Marie. "You were right about Aunt Lina's will. We think it might be connected to Angelo Bianchi."

Marie frowned.

"But how?"

"You know he was adopted, right?"

She nodded.

"I remember you mentioning it when we met some of their family at your graduation. It was obvious."

"There's a name in the will that we recognized, a Valarie Stokes. She has the same last name as the one who handled the adoption of Angelo."

"Valarie and Aunt Lina were best friends. You've met her

before, a few times," Marie told me, reminding me of why her last name had looked familiar. "Her mother Victoria Stokes and nana were friends back in the day."

"Wait..." Gaia moved closer. "Do you think she was Angelo's biological mother?"

"I've never heard of her having a baby or being pregnant at all but it could've happened before we were born. Maybe it was meant to be a secret since she would've given him up."

Fuck.

Was Angelo a goddamn Carter?

"Your father lied about the will and said he didn't know a Valarie, but if she was Lina's best friend then he knew her."

"Why is he always *our father* and not yours too?" Ally asked, rolling her eyes. "Whatever. I don't care about any of this. Dad has always been a liar, it's nothing new. That's why I stay clear of him."

She hugged Gaia again and then gave me one.

"I'm heading back to the party before mom sends a search party. Let's go, Marie."

She took Ree's hand and they left the room.

"Are you angry with me?" Gaia asked. "I said I wouldn't get into any trouble but I hate bullies."

I chuckled and took her hand.

"I'm not angry. I appreciate you for protecting my sister."

"I would do it again."

"Yeah? Does that mean you'll help me take out Marie's fiancé?"

Her eyes lit up and I knew I'd finally met my match, my partner in crime and love.

"It would be my pleasure, Mr. Carter."

I took her hand and led us out of the party, with eyes from guests including my father and mother on us. They wouldn't take my departure well but he could see me about it another day; I was banking on it.

I got Gaia home in record time, wanting to fulfill her requests to eat and be cuddled.

Truthfully, I needed her too.

"What's wrong, Rocco?" she asked softly, calling me by my nickname for the first time. "You're so gloomy."

She'd changed out of her gown and met me in the kitchen.

I hadn't realized that I was staring off into space until I heard her voice.

"Just thinking about my sister," I told her. "She's been suffering all this time while I was off living my life."

Gaia stepped in front of me and touched my cheek.

"I know you won't believe this but it isn't your fault that your father is a sick human being."

I leaned into her touch.

"He fucked us up. I always thought it was me more than them that he tortured, that if I stayed away it would make their lives easier but..."

"Nothing can stop a man like him from doing the things he does. Not you being away or here in the thick of his bullshit. You have to beat him at his own game, baby."

I pulled her against me and held on tight.

"These people don't deserve you," she whispered. "I'll kill them all to make you happy."

"You make me happy."

She sighed and backed away, her eyes taking me in slowly.

"What did he do to you? He did something, right? When you were younger?"

I shook my head and grabbed my phone to order food from a late night spot.

"Do you like Jamaican?" I asked, eyes on my screen.

"Um..." She cleared her throat. "Yes but will it be as good as Akira's cousin's spot in New York?"

I chuckled.

"It's just as good and they don't skimp on the portions."

I texted the owner instead of calling, knowing the old fool was working late with the rest of his staff.

Instead of asking Gaia what she wanted, I ordered half the menu and set my phone aside.

"I need you to do something for me."

I met her curious gaze.

"Anything," she answered without thinking about it.

"Find out who Pierson Hugh is."

"That'll be easy..." She smiled and turned to leave, but turned back and came to me. "You can trust me with your past, present, and future."

Then she took off without giving me time to process her words.

"Fuck," I muttered.

How was I supposed to tell her the truth?

CHAPTER 13

GAIA

"They're horrible people, Luci," I whispered, not wanting Rocco to hear. "All of them except his sisters and I hadn't been too sure about them at first either."

"I had no idea..." She sighed. "I always thought he and his family were close like ours. I mean Enzo had told me a while ago that he and his dad had a strained relationship but I didn't think it was that bad."

I laid back and stared up at the ceiling. After gathering all the information I could on Pierson, I decided to give Rocco time to think.

He would find me when the food was here, but I knew he needed a moment.

His family were a broken bunch and I hated it.

I wanted to fix it, *for him.*

He needed it and my heart wouldn't let me rest until he had peace of mind.

"I don't know how to fix it."

"You can't fix it, G. If they're broken it's probably years of trauma and mistreatment involved. That's not something you can easily mend."

I rolled over and covered my head with the thick duvet, tears pricking the corners of my eyes.

"Are you crying?" she asked, sounding more distressed than I felt.

"No," I lied, wiping my eyes. "Okay, yes. He's hurting. I can feel it and I want to make it better."

"My soft baby," she murmured. "Do you remember when we were kids and you would get upset at Luca for stepping on ants."

I smiled.

"He did it on purpose. They weren't bothering anyone."

"Luca was meant to be a menace. But, I'm saying this because we've always known you were a softy at heart, G. You care about people and their feelings and your goal is to make the world better for women. It's what makes you, *you*. I never want you to change that because it reminds me not to lose myself in this life. You don't have to say it but I know you struggled with being by my side all these years and I love you so much for doing it. Whenever you want out, all you have to do is say the word. Luca and I will understand."

She knew how bad I needed to hear that and it eased a little of my guilt.

"I don't know what I want."

Lucia laughed.

"Maybe not everything but I think you have a solid stance on at least one thing... *or person*."

I buried myself deeper, hiding my face as if she could see me.

"Don't tease me!"

Her laughter filled the line and it made me happy, even in my embarrassment.

"As long as you're happy, so am I."

"I want him to be happy, too," I murmured, really meaning it.

"I told you already that you make me happy," Rocco said, scaring the shit out of me.

I popped out from under the blanket with wide eyes.

"You were eavesdropping!"

He smirked and walked over to my side of the bed.

"I only heard that last part. Came to tell you that our food was here..." He looked down at my phone and pointed. "That Lucia?"

I nodded and he reached for it, placing it to his ear.

"We're gonna call you back."

He ended the call and pulled me out of bed.

"Come on. I need to feed and cuddle you."

With his fingers wrapped around mine, he led us over to the elevator.

We went up instead of down and I eyed him closely as we sat down in the living area and ate our food.

"If you keep staring I won't be able to focus on eating," he said, glancing over with a smirk lifting the corners of his mouth.

I set my oxtail platter down and slid close to him, wanting to soak up his presence some more.

"What's up, Shortcake? Speak your mind."

"Pierson Hugh isn't anyone important on paper," I said, revealing my findings. "He's been a senior accountant at the same firm for owner a decade. It gives me the impression that he's into something illegal."

Rocco nodded, he held his fork out to my lips with rice and peas piled on it.

"An easy target," he mused, feeding me. "Do we have an address?"

I lifted an eyebrow.

"What kind of question is that? I have his address, the code to his security system and layout of his home."

He shook his head with a smile playing on his lips.

"Do I want to know how you got the code to his system?"

I shrugged. "Probably not."

Rocco continued to feed me his food and I let him, relishing in the way he babied me.

When both his platter and mine were empty, he bagged up the rest of the food and lifted me off the couch.

"What's up with you picking me up?"

"You like it, don't play coy with me."

He carried me into his bedroom and fell into bed with me clutched tightly in his arms.

"I was supposed to be cuddling the anger out of you but we missed that opportunity."

I adjusted myself until my body was stretched out on top of his.

"My anger went away with the offer to handle Marie's fiancé."

His fingers danced along my spine, down the curve of my ass and back, over and over until it opened the floodgates between my thighs.

The gentle way in which he touched me was enough to make me crazy about him.

"Earlier you asked about what my dad did to me growing up and—"

I propped myself up on his chest.

"You don't have to talk about it if you're not ready."

"He was abusive," he confessed, his eyes on mine. "It was only mentally at first. He would call me sensitive for crying or showing emotion, and as a kid I didn't understand why I couldn't do those things."

My heart ached for a young Ricardo.

"The older I got I think he was threatened by my size. I started playing football as an outlet and bulked up a little."

"He hit you?"

"He did a lot of bad things to me."

I could feel that he was still holding back, that whatever his father had done to him he wasn't over it.

"Does your mom know?"

"I don't see how she couldn't have but we've never talked about it."

I pushed myself up and straddled him, overwhelmed by what he was telling me.

"I'm so sorry no one protected you, Rocco."

He looked away.

"I learned how to protect myself."

"But you shouldn't have had to..." I cupped his face, forcing him to look at me. "I'll never let anybody hurt you again."

Maybe it wouldn't hold as much weight, because he was bigger and stronger and people feared him now, but there wasn't a soul who could stop me from killing them over this man.

He was embedded inside of me, in my heart.

I leaned in and kissed his forehead, then his nose and lips, while rolling my hips against his growing erection. Now that we'd crossed that line, I couldn't and wouldn't let up.

"Take those off," he whispered, tugging at my shorts. "I want you to ride me slow and don't look away until you come on my dick."

Feining to give him what he wanted, I quickly got out of my shorts and removed his too.

His dick had no right to be this long and thick and my pussy loved the sweet pain it brought as he stretched me out in order to fill me up our first time.

I stroked him with two hands, eyes never leaving his.

"Stop fucking playing with me and sit on it," he growled, pulling me forward.

He produced an unopened condom we'd left on the bed from the night before and I ripped the package open, lifting up to secure it on him.

After pinching the tip I gradually lowered myself, feeling proud of the way my walls had already molded to fit his size.

"Uhh," I whimpered after taking him in all the way. "Do you feel that?"

Our gazes clashed and he nodded.

"Made for me," he murmured, gripping my hips and thrusting up into me.

I used his chest to balance myself and got up on the souls of my feet.

He moaned softly and it fueled my need to fuck him senseless.

Lifting up, I rode the tip, tightening my walls as I worked the head.

"Don't look away," I instructed, reminding him of his request before his eyes drifted shut. "I want to see how much you enjoy this pussy."

He pushed his hands beneath my thighs and leveled me in the air before fucking me deep me with swift upstrokes. I wanted so badly to fuck back but my body was buzzing from the assault on my g-spot from this angle, I could barely breathe.

On the verge of cumming and wanting more time, I dropped to my knees and pressed my chest and forehead to his.

Skin on skin, eyes locked, I ground into him fast and hard-- twisting my hips to keep him buried deep.

"I love the way you feel inside of me," I whispered against his lips.

He slapped my ass and drew his legs up, stiffening his hips while I rode his dick.

"Keep riding my shit just like that," he breathed, digging his fingers in the skin of my waist. "Fuck, you feel so damn good."

I whimpered, losing myself in the way he clung to me.

How could a man who'd been so cold when we first met, be so needy when we're fucking? His hands were all over, sliding up and down my back, squeezing my ass and waist, like he was silently begging me to never let go.

My heart wanted nothing more than to give him everything he needed.

"Ricardo," I moaned, nipping at his bottom lip as he fucked me harder.

It hurt so damn good.

The combination of his strokes and the beautiful sounds our bodies were making, skin slapping skin while my pussy sang his praises, was like nothing I'd ever experienced before.

"I'm about to cum," I cried.

He enclosed both hands around my neck and asked, "Do you trust me?"

I nodded, willing to surrender all power to him my trust was so deep.

He squeezed and my core tightened the harder it became to breathe.

All of my senses were heightened, my body filled with tingles that grew more intense between my legs the longer he forced me to hold out.

Our gazes were locked in an intense stare down and I saw myself in him again.

This time it was different.

His eyes were soulless but filled with promise.

His cold demeanor had softened.

He cared and was gentle, loving.

"Mmhm," he hummed, coaching me through my revelation. "Let it go for me."

He released my neck a fraction, giving me room to breathe and as I let air into my lungs I shattered around him.

"I want to be the reason you breathe," he confessed through his orgasm. "You've already become mine."

Those were the last words I heard before falling into a deep sleep.

My alarm woke us at three in the morning and I was grateful to have set one.

We dressed in silence, both in our heads about what needed to be done for his sister.

Or maybe... maybe we were thinking about how to breathe for the other.

Was it crazy to want such a thing from another human being?

Rocco led me into his workout room and then into the closet where a large safe sat.

Inside were enough weapons to man a small army.

"Wyatt sent a few men over to sit on Pierson's place. There hasn't been any movement other than him arriving home from the party alone."

I leaned against the door frame and watched him load the clip on a pretty Glock 9.

"Is that registered?"

"What kind of criminal do you take me as?" he asked, sounding offended.

"It's too pretty not to be..." I moved to stand behind him and peeked around his body. "Look at the detail in the metal."

I slid my finger over the mix of Matte and gloss.

"This was custom made. Where'd you get it?"

He shrugged and put it back, grabbing another piece to take instead.

"Everything in here came from the O'Sullivans."

I nodded.

"Makes sense. They import their weapons from Ireland. I want one."

He waved to the safe.

"What's mine is yours. Pick what you want out of it later..." He glanced at his phone after concealing his gun. "Our ride is here."

Down in the garage was a dark colored impala waiting for us.

Manny stepped out and stretched, his eyes meeting mine after a second.

"She's coming?" he asked.

"Why are you asking him when I'm standing right here?" I queried, brows furrowed.

"You—" He scratched his head. "Are you coming to hack something?"

Rocco laughed and opened the back door.

"Come on, Shortcake. Get in. I'll sit back here with you."

Manny looked confused and I realized his cousin hadn't told him anything about me or maybe Wyatt only knew me as a hacker too.

With a smirk, I slid into the backseat.

This should be fun.

CHAPTER 14
ROCCO

"Shouldn't she stay in the car?" Manny asked quietly so Gaia wouldn't hear.

I opened my mouth to warn him about the stupid shit he said out of his mouth at times, but it was too late. From behind, Gaia pressed her thumbs into the soft tissue at the base of his neck.

"Ah, fuck!" he groaned, falling into the car.

Luckily, Pierson lived in a secluded area where the homes were far apart and a little noise wouldn't attract any attention.

"The next time you say something sexist out of your mouth, I'm going to skin you alive," she threatened, twirling her knife in his face.

His eyes met mine and I shrugged.

"Never judge a book by its cover, Manny. You know this."

"You could've told me she was crazy..." He scoffed and stood tall, recovering quickly. "I like it."

"Don't like it too much," I warned as Gaia pulled out a device that looked like an old school cellphone.

She sat it on the hood of the car and connected it to her phone.

"What does that do?" Manny asked, leaning forward to get a good look.

"My phone has a mirror server attached and will help it keep power. It'll jam any cameras and phone lines in the area and I'll be able to disarm his security system from it."

Manny nodded, his gaze following her hand movements.

"Teach me your ways."

She cut her eyes at him.

"If you're serious, then yes. But it takes a lot of practice and coding to do what I do."

He looked like a fucking school kid eager to learn.

"Yes, ma'am."

She smiled and punched in a twelve digit sequence after the device powered on.

After a few seconds, she nodded.

"We're good to go."

Manny took off and I pulled Gaia into me to distract her from following behind him.

"Why does he get to go first?" she asked, looking over her shoulder as he disappeared into the shadows.

"He's an efficient sweeper. I can't let you go in until I have the all clear."

She wrapped her arms around me and squeezed.

"Thank you for being my protector," she whispered into my chest as Manny gave the signal.

"Always..." I kissed her forehead. "Let's go."

We moved through the bushes to get into Pierson's yard.

His security system had automatic lights but Gaia had done more than disarm the alarm, she'd shut down the power too.

Manny flashed a light from where he stood and we made our way over, slipping into the large home through a side door.

"He's sleeping upstairs. I have two guys watching the outside for movement."

Gaia was on the move before he could finish his spiel, her steps light as she took the winding stairwell to the top floor.

"Time to wake up, Pierson," Gaia cooed as she hopped on the bed and dropped into a squat.

Moving around to the side he slept on, I pointed my gun at his head.

Pierson's snores echoed over her command and she sighed before slapping him in the face.

They always slept good when causing havoc in somebody else's life.

"I said wake the fuck up!"

He jumped and got tangled in the blanket.

After feeling the barrel of my gun on his forehead, he stilled.

"W-What is t-this?" he asked, barely able to get his words out.

The moonlight from his balcony door lit the room up enough for him to see us.

"Let's talk," Gaia said, sitting cross legged now.

"A-About what?"

"About how you get to die. It can be easy or not, but that's up to you."

He looked between me and Gaia, repeatedly.

"There's no way out of this, Pierson Hugh. Senior accountant at Kellen and Beck. You're an only child, your parents are dead, you've never been married. No kids..." Gaia *tsked* as she listed off the shit she knew about him. "I think we all know you couldn't—even in your prime—bag a woman like Marie Carter. So, tell me, what did her father offer you?"

He took a breath, almost as if he'd accepted his fate.

"I handle his money," he confessed. "For the last two years, his deposits have been *different.* Not above board."

"And you thought marrying my sister would get you what?" I asked, shoving the gun into his mouth. "It doesn't matter. You fucked up the minute you put fear in her eyes."

I watched that same look build in his until I was satisfied.

"Did he offer a marriage pact to keep you quiet?"

He nodded and I scoffed.

"He was better off putting a bullet in your head," I groused, snatching my gun back. "Where are your files?"

"I-In the office down the hall in a safe. T-The key is taped under the desk."

It was apparent that Pierson wasn't the kind of man you went into business with, let alone hand your daughter over to.

Pussy.

"Good boy," Gaia said, jumping off the bed. "I'll go handle that..." She got to the door and turned. "Men like you disgust me. I hope you burn for an eternity."

I waited until she was gone and nodded for Manny to step forward.

"You're Ricardo, right?" Pierson asked, suddenly finding his voice. "We can work this out. I'll call off the wedding and apologize to your sister for dragging her into it. I—"

I tipped my head, watching him switch into survival mode now that Gaia was in the other room.

"And the apology for leaving marks on her skin?" I asked coolly.

He nodded animatedly.

"Y-Yes I can do that."

I chuckled and scratched my forehead with the butt of my gun.

"You have no idea who the fuck I am, do you?"

His eyes darted to Manny who was filling a syringe with a calcium based concoction to send him into cardiac arrest.

He sat up straighter and I leaned in.

"My father never tells the whole truth and now you have to die because of it. Be grateful, I can't play with you how I want. Be *very* fucking grateful."

My fingers itched to pull the trigger instead, but I had to play my cards right.

He was connected to my father and being attached to him in any way would bring a story if he went missing or was found bloodied and bruised.

What mattered was my sister wouldn't suffer a fate she didn't ask for.

And if my father decided to pin another man on her I'd kill that muthafucka too.

"Put 'em to sleep, Manny."

I walked away before I did something I would regret.

Gaia was already in the hall with a bag slung over her shoulders, back against the wall.

"I know walking away was hard," she said. "I'm proud of you."

Her words did something to me, to my fucking heart.

"Proud of me?"

She nodded.

"Yeah. Is that okay? For me to be proud of you for walking away to keep the people you love safe from scrutiny?"

"And what about when I can't show restraint, then what?"

"I'll be there to help you fix it," she said without pause. "I just wanted you to know that I have your back."

We stood in silence after that, staring at one another.

I had a new found appreciation for Gaia and the way she handled me with care.

"If you two are done with this sappy ass moment, we can

go," Manny interrupted as he stepped into the hall. "Somebody needs to feed me for getting up at the ass crack of dawn."

Gaia chuckled and we followed him down the stairs.

"You're like a six year old," she said as we left and locked up like we hadn't been there.

Manny took the gloves we wore and bagged them to be burned.

"A hungry six year old," he grumbled, clearly in a mood.

"I'll cook dinner tonight and you're more than welcome to join, but you're on your own for breakfast, Kid."

He shot a smirk in my direction before we slid into the impala and said, "She loves me."

"Keep it up and I'll chopped your fingers off right before dinner is served and eat in your face while you bleed out," I threatened.

That's just mean," he complained as we got out of dodge.

Gaia wasn't the only one in this relationship that would clear a town if a man even looked at her too long.

Manny was joking, he'd always been a flirt, but she was mine and I was the only man who could flirt with her.

And I mean that shit.

"What time will dinner be ready?" Manny asked after pulling into the garage.

"Six sharp and if you're late I will not let you in," Gaia told him, patting his head. "You can invite Wyatt but the same applies to him. Are the two of you allergic to anything?"

He turned in his seat and smiled at her.

"Aww, you care enough to ask, but no."

She nodded and got out.

I waited until the door closed to address him.

"Appreciate you," I told him.

He waved me off.

"Anything for Ree, but when Lacey calls to cash in on the

161

favor I had to offer in order to get that calcium concoction, it's on you to fulfill it."

Lacey was his sister.

She worked in a hospital.

I was surprised she hadn't been caught yet doing half the shit Wyatt and Manny asked of her, but she'd always been smooth as hell, and able to get out of anything with the gift of gab she'd been blessed with.

"I ain't got no problem with that..." I pushed my door open. "Aye, don't be late. If you offend her, it'll offend me."

He chuckled and I almost cursed myself for sounding like fucking Matteo.

I met Gaia inside and she insisted on checking the fridge for what to cook before heading up to shower and get more sleep.

"Oh, there's sirloin in here," she exclaimed excitedly. "I'll make pepper steak and rice. That's a quick and easy dish but will fill everyone up."

I admired how excited she was to cook for my friends.

"Would it be cool if I invite my sisters? I need to tell Ree the news anyway."

She turned and walked toward me after setting the frozen meat in the sink.

"Of course, I was going to ask but you beat me to it."

I leaned against the island and pulled her into me.

"Yeah?"

"Mmhm," she hummed, resting her head in my chest. "Your family is my family now, too. As long as they're good to you then I'll be good to them."

That meant the world to me.

"Happy to hear that, Shortcake."

"Oh!" She danced a little and went to the pantry. "Speaking of shortcakes. I haven't had one in days."

I watched her pull one from the box, rip the wrapper off, and devour it in three bites.

"We need to work on your eating habits, mama."

She took another out the box and waved it at me.

"You can take everything else away but not these, promise me!"

I chuckled.

Gaia was dramatic and silly and sweet and greedy as fuck, but mostly she was mine.

"I promise not to take them away from you."

She nodded and tore open another one, satisfied with my response.

After biting half, she offered me the rest.

I beckoned her, pretending to want it.

"Kiss me and let me taste what's in your mouth."

Never expecting her to do it, she lifted up on her tiptoes, stuck her tongue in my mouth and swirled it around until all I could taste was that damn cake.

"Fuck, my dick is hard now."

I pressed my erection into her stomach and she giggled before leaving me hanging.

"Come upstairs and I'll take care of that for you."

I followed without needing to be told twice.

There was no turning back now, we'd opened a door that could never be closed, unless we were both on the other side.

Just how it should be.

Later that evening, Gaia dressed in a pair of light blue jeans and sheer black blouse.

I watched her loosen her hair from the buns she'd worn to the gala and fluff her frizzy curls out.

"Wear it like that," I said from my spot on the bed. "I like when it's wild."

"Me too but you'll have to help me wash it later or it'll be a tangled mess soon."

I nodded and walked up behind her, taking the necklace she was trying to clasp and doing it for her.

"You always wear this one," I pointed out, wanting to know the significance.

She smiled and rolled the heart pendant between her fingers while watching me through the mirror.

"My dad gave it to me on my eight birthday. He knew he could protect me best in Philly but that anything could happen if one of his enemies decided to use me as collateral. It has a tracker inside."

I nodded.

"Do you feel safer?"

"Yes..." She tipped her head and turned. "You don't think it's to feel safe from you, right?"

"Nah, that never crossed my mind. Just wondering if we should put trackers on one another in the future."

"You'd let me track you?"

"Hell, yeah, I would. If anybody can find me, it's you."

She smiled, clearly proud of herself.

"As long as you know. I'd search heaven and earth for you, Ricardo."

We stared at one another and then broke into laughter.

"That was so fucking corny, Shortcake. But I fucks with it."

"I know but I still mean it."

"As long as you know, I'll do the same for you."

"I know. Now come on before your friend shows up and sees I haven't started cooking yet."

"He'll be alright. The muthafucka is lucky I'm allowing him to eat at all. He's like a cat, feed him once and he'll keep coming back."

We made it down into the kitchen just as my phone alerted me to someone entering the garage.

I checked the code used and decided to meet Marie down there so we could talk.

"I'll be right back. I want to holla at Ree for a second alone."

Gaia nodded and busied herself with dinner.

"Oh, hey," Ree greeted as the elevator door opened and I was inside. "You didn't have to come down. I—"

"It'll probably be a while before they find him, but you don't have to worry about marrying anybody anymore."

She stood rooted in place, her gaze pinned to mine as if she were trying to hold back tears. And sure enough they fell, breaking my heart but also filling me with relief.

"Come here, Ree."

I pulled her into me and she cried harder than I think I'd ever seen from her.

She'd always been the *tough* one but I knew deep down she didn't want that title. It was hard to break yourself out of something forced down your throat.

"Next time you feel backed into a corner, call me. I'll always come running for you."

She clung to me for a little while longer and pulled away, wiping the evidence of her little moment away.

"Thank you," she whispered. "I owe you."

I waved her off.

"You're my sister. I don't want shit from you but for us to be close like before, without you shoving being a family with dad down my throat."

She nodded.

"Fuck him," she griped. "He's a sorry excuse for a father, always has been."

"You good now?"

"Yeah, I'm good..." We stepped into the elevator. "So, and don't get offended by this, but can Gaia cook? Because we both know you can't boil water."

I tossed my head and laughed.

"Aye, fuck you..." I shoved her. "I'm not sure though. She's never cooked for me before, but her family throws these big ass Sunday dinners once a month. Her mom and aunt can throw down."

"You've met her mother?" she asked as the elevator doors opened on the first floor.

"Not officially but yeah."

Gaia lifted her head at the sound of my voice and smiled.

"Hey, Ree. How are you feeling?" she asked, returning to chop veggies like a pro.

"I'm good. Just wondering if we should have a few pizza orders on standby."

Gaia chuckled, tapping the tip of the knife against the cutting board like it really tickled her.

"Don't worry. I know what I'm doing, so there's no need for pizza."

They started to chat, Ree mostly asking Gaia a million and one questions about herself.

And eventually my place was bustling with Ally, Wyatt, and Manny.

It was the first time I had so many people in my home at once and it was all because of her. She brought us together and I saw this group here as our own little family.

For a short moment, my heart was full.

But then the elevator chimed and my mother walked in with an attitude that changed my mood.

"What is this?" she asked, looking around as if someone had betrayed her. "I've called you multiple times..." She looked at my sisters who had both stopped eating at the sight of her.

"And you two, only to find you all here purposely ignoring me."

I moved in her direction.

"No one was ignoring you."

"Sorry, Ms. Deidre," Gaia chimed in, trying to save the day. "In my family, when we share melas together we sometimes cut our phones off to enjoy the moment. I suggested we do that while eating tonight, I apologize."

"This ain't your family, little girl."

Before Gaia could respond, I stepped in.

"Ma, don't come in my shit talking to her like you don't have sense. She's not your child nor is she a little girl. That's a grown ass woman."

She reared back like I'd slapped her and I sighed, annoyed with her presence.

"You can go and don't come back until you learn some fucking manners, especially where I pay bills."

She scoffed.

"How can you speak to me that way? I'm your mother."

"Telling me you're my mother doesn't change my mind."

"I came here to tell you something important and instead you're having a little family dinner with barely any family here."

"Damn, Mrs. Carter I thought you liked me," Manny mumbled loud enough for her to hear but she ignored him.

"You left your father's gala for that girl and now you're excluding your own parents from your life."

I walked past her and hit the call button on the elevator.

"Let's go," I demanded, waving for her to get inside.

One thing about this lady, she could ruin your fucking mood without trying too hard.

She was selfish and manipulative and I was sick of the bullshit.

Anybody else would be dead talking to Gaia like that, but my mother would have to get a different kind of treatment to settle my anger.

She got inside reluctantly and I followed her.

As the doors closed, she started up again but I wasn't hearing it.

"Let me tell you something..." I backed her into a corner and her eyes widened. "And I need you to hear me good cause I won't be repeating myself. If you ever disrespect my woman where *we* lay our heads or anywhere else for that matter, we're done. You can kiss this half assed relationship goodbye and I mean that shit with everything in me."

The doors opened and I stepped back.

"Go home and that'll be the last time you get in with a code. Your shit has been revoked."

She stood stunned on the other side as I hit the button to shut the doors in her face.

Night fucking ruined.

CHAPTER 15
GAIA

Two more laps.

I pushed myself to the limit, needing the stress I felt to fall off my shoulders sooner rather than later.

Rocco had been in a mood since his mother showed up to our dinner a week ago. He was distant and cold and I had no idea what to do to make it better.

It was eating me up inside, because I knew he needed me but didn't know how to convey his feelings without looking *too sensitive.*

His mother was a walking contradiction; how could you love your children but treat them like they don't mean shit to you. How do you allow them to be harmed and used by their father?

How could she stay married and continue to turn a blind eye to his bullshit?

My skin burned thinking about it all.

She was just as bad as her disrespectful ass husband. I wanted nothing more than to chain him up and carve my name into his body.

"*Shit*," I cursed, coming to a stop to catch my breath.

I placed my hands on my head and shut my eyes, willing my body to cool down.

It took a while but eventually the heavy breathing stopped and I grabbed my things, fully prepared to go back home and coerce Rocco into talking to me. Whatever I had to do, I would do it.

With my mind on him, it took longer to notice that the guard who usually worked the front desk had been replaced by someone else. I'd only been a couple of times in the last two and a half weeks, but something about this man's presence didn't feel right.

"Have a good night, Ms. Wilson," he called as I reached the door.

I stopped moving and glanced over my shoulder to find that he'd stood up.

"Yeah..." I nodded. "Thanks."

Focusing forward, I watched him through the door and wrapped my fingers around the handle of my gun inside of my bag.

The silence heightened my senses as I stepped out into a snowstorm.

Great.

Across the parking lot, leaning against the car I borrowed from Rocco was a man I hadn't seen before. I approached until about halfway and then stopped, tipping my head in question.

"I come in peace," he said, standing tall.

"Doesn't feel that way," I quipped, brandishing my gun.

He held his hands up and took a step forward.

"I think it's best for you to stand there if you come in peace," I warned, stepping back on my right foot. "I'm in a mood to shoot something tonight."

He smiled a little and it reminded me of Rocco.

I frowned and looked him over; he was sort of built like him but more on the lanky side.

His eyes were dark with that same cold look dancing in them but there was a softness to him that made me a relax a little.

"Do you see it yet?" he asked, looking around as if someone would jump out and catch us.

I dropped my arms, gun still clutched in my hand.

"You're his brother, aren't you?"

He nodded.

"Is that your guy in there?"

Another nod.

"Did you kill the guard who was on duty?"

"Nah but your boy will when he finds out I paid him to take a little break."

He was being sincere, my gut told me so but his presence didn't make sense.

"Why are you here?"

He stuffed his hands in the pockets of his jeans.

"Only you can get him to meet with me..." He took a step forward. "I'm not here to harm you or him. There's something he should know."

I put my gun away and closed the distance between us.

"What's your name?"

He pulled a hand from his pocket and pushed it in my direction.

There was an insignia tattooed on his hand, a crown with only three points and an H underneath. I recognized it as the daughter of a Gang member.

Correction, as the daughter of the head of a gang.

"Harlem," he said. "Harlem Carter."

I took his hand and looked him in the eyes.

"You're the head of the Three Kings."

He lifted an eyebrow.

"You know your organizations."

I released his hand and nodded.

"I know a thing or two."

If he didn't already know who my father was, I damn sure wouldn't be the one to tell him. With nothing left to talk about, I moved around him toward the driver's side.

"I'll see what I can do about Rocco. Be safe out here, Harlem."

I opened my door and quickly slid in.

Through the rearview, I watched him swagger away inside. A few minutes later, an illegally tinted G-Wagon pulled out from the side of the building and left the parking lot.

Once I felt that they were gone, I went back in to settle something.

The security guard who should've been at the desk when I left was back and lifted his head to speak but stopped at the sight of me.

"Ms--"

I saddled up to the lifted counter and leaned over it.

"The next time you put my life in danger for a quick buck, it won't be Ricardo you have to deal with. I'm the one you should fear from now on."

He nodded slowly.

"Use your fucking words before I change my mind about giving you grace."

"Y-Yes, o-of course."

"Good..." I nodded and smiled. "That's smart of you."

When I got back to Rocco's, I went up to his floor and found him standing on the terrace watching the snow fall.

He didn't acknowledge my presence but I didn't need him to.

Approaching from behind, I wrapped my arms around his waist and rested my head against his back.

"How was your run?" he asked, caressing my hands.

"Interesting."

He tugged me in front of him and lifted my head.

"How so?"

I wasn't sure how he would react to me being accosted by his half-brother and took my time responding.

"Shortcake..."

"I met your brother," I told him.

The expression in his eyes went from contemplative to murderous.

"Hey..." I gripped his face firmly. "Take a breather. He came in peace."

He pulled my hand away and took a step back.

"Him stepping to you at all is a problem, Gaia."

It felt like he'd slapped me in my face by using my name with so much force.

Taken into account that he was already in a bad mood, I decided to let it slide.

"You're right..." I closed the distance he put between us. "He shouldn't have come to me but he did and it's done."

He took a deep breath and nodded.

"Harlem, right?" he questioned, still stiff but less angry.

I nodded.

"He seems to think I can convince you to meet up with him. From what I can tell, whatever he needs to say was important enough for him to seek me out."

His fingers brushed my arms and he lifted one, eyeing the goosebumps doting my skin.

It was cold out but I would stand in the cold with him if he needed it.

"Let's go inside. You're cold."

I shook my head.

"I'm okay. I'd rather be here with you."

Instead of listening, he pulled me through the terrace door and into the heat.

"Did you know he was the head of the Three Kings?" I asked, earning a sideways glance from Rocco who had grabbed a blanket to drape over my arms.

"Did he tell you that?"

"There's a tattoo on his hand—a crown with three points and the first initial in his name underneath."

He looked perplexed by the revelation.

"You didn't know," I surmised, waving the blanket away. "I need to shower."

His gaze dropped to my exposed stomach.

"I need to buy you workout clothes with more fabric."

I rolled my eyes and moved to push past him.

"Nah..." He grabbed my arm and lifted me off the floor. "Shower up here."

"I need to grab—"

"I'll get it," he cut in, walking into his bedroom and then the bathroom. "I want you to stay up here with me from now on."

I crossed my arms, feeling defiant.

"I didn't think you wanted me to."

He turned after cutting the shower for me.

"Why wouldn't I want that?"

"You've been distant with me. I don't want to invade your space when it seems you—"

He kissed me softly and I hated how easily I melted into him. More than that, I hated how hungry I was for this man.

He hadn't kissed me in a week.

Hugged me.

Smiled for me.

Nothing.

I felt deprived of the best parts of him, the parts he didn't show anyone else.

"Invade my space," he murmured against my lips. "Suffocate me. Love on me. I need you."

His words settled my worried heart.

"I just thought..."

I shook my head.

"I know and that's my bad. I've been lost in my head this week."

"Okay..." I caressed his face. "Will you come back and sit with me while I shower?"

His hands found their way to my ass.

"I can do that..." He turned me toward the shower. "Get in and I'll be back."

By the time he returned, I had drenched my body in water and lathered up with some unscented soap. Sliding the glass door back, he handed over my exfoliating gloves and favorite moisturizing body wash.

"Thank you."

I could feel his eyes on me as I turned around to continue my shower.

"You can come in if you want," I offered, glancing over my shoulder. "But you have to use these gloves and help with my back."

He mumbled something before I heard clothes hitting the floor. A few seconds later, his fingers were grazing my skin as he entered the shower.

"I'm sorry I've been distant," he murmured, kissing the spot just below my ear. "I missed you in my bed and my arms, Shortcake."

I was grateful to be facing away from him because my smile wouldn't subside quickly enough.

"It's okay for you to need space," I told him. "Sometimes I get in my head too and need time to work my way out of it."

He took the gloves from my hand and slipped them on, mumbling something about them feeling weird before responding to what I'd said.

"I'm always in my head," he admitted, picking up the body wash and pouring a generous amount into his palm. "Trying not to be seen."

He worked his hands into a good lather and started on my shoulders.

"You should want to be seen."

He shook his head.

"Nah, I'd rather not."

I hated what his parents turned him into, what he felt like he had to be in order to survive.

"But, I see you, Ricardo. Do you not want that?"

Instead of responding, he twirled his finger—signaling me to turn so he could get my back.

I obliged and kept quiet while he finished.

As the silence prolonged, I began to feel weighed down with emotion.

Maybe he didn't want that, at least not completely.

"You can rinse," he said, breaking the silence.

I got the soap off my body and switched positions with him so he could shower next.

Briefly, I waited with him. Even though he'd said he wanted me to invade his space, I didn't feel welcomed anymore.

"I'll get out now and dry off," I whispered, my stupid eyes filling with tears.

Get it together!

"Don't leave this shower, Gaia Juliette."

His tone, while slightly harsh, made me want to suck his dick.

I was out of my mind.

"Ricardo..."

He turned and my gaze dropped, taking in how hard he'd gotten.

"Yeah, baby?"

Back again was that soft cadence I think he only reserved for me.

"What's your middle name?"

He chuckled and backed me against the shower wall.

"Would you believe me if I told you I didn't have one?"

I frowned.

"Really?"

He nodded and caged me in with his hands.

"Ree and Ally don't either. Not sure why, never cared enough to ask."

I hummed and brushed my fingers down his chest.

"Your family is so odd."

"Tell me about it," he moaned softly as I wrapped my hand around his dick and stroked it softly.

"You hurt my feelings," I admitted, stroking him faster.

He closed his eyes and rested his forehead against mine.

"I'm...I'm sorry, baby."

I added my other hand and worked them in different directions, twisting and pulling until he was hard as a fucking brick in my hands.

His breathing picked up and the moans came next.

He sounded so fucking sexy.

"Why are you sorry? Mm?"

"For being distan--*shit*."

I shook my head and slowed down, wanting to torture him until he got it right.

"Try again and I'll speed up."

"Fuck, woman. I can't think straight."

I laughed, my pussy wet with excitement.

Maybe it was the power I had over him in this moment, the power he was so freely giving me.

"You can do it."

I dropped a hand and he growled, nipping at my neck.

"I want you to see me," he said after second. "I want... Fuckk, keep doing that."

I added my hand back and jerked him off faster, swiping my thumbs over the tip with the intentions of driving him absolutely crazy.

"I need you to see me," he moaned with conviction, thrusting his hips to get more from me.

I dropped to my knees and opened my mouth, peering up at him.

"Put it in my mouth and fuck my throat," I demanded, playing with my pussy.

He obliged with glee, slipping his dick between my lips while holding on to the shower wall. I swallowed and took him further, crying at how good my fingers felt--at how beautiful he looked standing over me like a fucking god.

I was his to do as he pleased with.

"You nasty fucking slut," he moaned, snatching my head back by my hair. "I'll a kill a muthafucka about you."

My clit throbbed so hard it hurt.

I slapped it over and over while fingering myself.

Barely able to see him through my watery eyes, I took the dick he dropped in my mouth repeatedly like a champ. I'd never let a man do this to me, but something about *this man* filled me with the urge to do all kinds of shit.

"Ah," I cried around the strokes as I came.

"Fuckkkk," he growled, cumming down my throat and then pulling out to release the rest on my mouth and chin.

I licked it off and smiled.

"Mm, you taste good."

Rocco pulled me up and smashed his lips against mine.

"Woman, what the fuck was that?" he questioned.

I smiled and looked away, feeling shy all of sudden.

"Nah, don't do that."

"I wanted to experience something different with you," I admitted.

He kissed me again and then buried his face in my neck, sucking on the flesh softly.

Out of nowhere I thought about the guard at the track.

If I didn't tell him and he found out from Harlem first, all hell would break loose.

Luckily his inhibitions were lowered, so, I said, "There's something else you should know about my run tonight."

He looked up, his chest still heaving from cuming hard, brows furrowed.

"What is it?"

CHAPTER 16
ROCCO

"What did I hire you for?" I asked, watching JP struggle to get out the hog tie I placed him in. "You had *one* job and you failed me."

Shaking my head, I kneeled and lifted his head with the barrel of my gun.

"What did I tell you would happen if something happened to her?"

He tried speaking through the gag and I lowered it.

"H-He said he was your brother," he explained, eyes wet with tears. "I thought—"

I stood and placed the sole of my Timbs against his neck, slowly applying pressure.

"Wrong," I finished for him. "You thought wrong."

The sound of heavy footfalls approached from behind and I pointed my gun in that direction without turning.

"You got five minutes to get whatever you need off your chest, Harlem."

I released JP and slowly gave my half-brother my attention.

The same eyes we shared with our father met mine.

I couldn't deny him as kin even if I'd wanted to. We didn't have a relationship but had known about one another since fifteen and fourteen.

He was one year younger than me, born just five months before Allyson.

Though there had always been suspicions of other children, Harlem was indeed a Carter.

"I'm surprised your girl is gonna let you kill him."

I wanted to laugh but I was in a mood.

Even so, he wasn't wrong.

Gaia had made me promise to only rough him up because he made a *mistake.*

She knew as well as I did that mistakes are what got people killed. One wrong decision or move and shit could go left.

But her caring nature wouldn't allow me to take a life for something so *trivial.*

Fucking woman.

Four minutes now," I said, reminding him of his time.

He chuckled and dropped down into a squat, his eyes on a nervous JP.

"Nice knots," he mused to himself. "Sorry, I got you in trouble, Kid. Think of it as a life lesson. All money ain't good money and sometimes people like me lie to get what they want."

His honesty intrigued me.

It reminded me of myself.

"Rocco," he said addressing me as he stood. "We don't have a relationship but we have a common enemy."

He stepped toward me, his eyes meeting mine.

"Our father is a bitch," he went on, never breaking eye contact. "Always has been, always will be."

I nodded.

"That why you here? To talk about Robert?"

"I'm here to warn you about his plans to skip the country after he's removed from office for judicial misconduct."

Though what he was revealing was news to me, I didn't expect anything less from my father.

Years of abusing his power had finally caught up to him.

"That's only after he transfers some of the blame to our mothers."

The *fuck*.

"Elaborate."

"Now I have more than five minutes?"

I ignored his smug attitude and walked around him to cut JP loose.

"Take a week off and return with a better understanding of our agreement."

He got himself up and left through the alley door, stumbling on his way out.

I waited until the door slammed shut before addressing Harlem again.

"Who's your source?"

"I'm my own source," he lied, protecting his asset same as I would. "He's been under investigation for the last year and the media will catch wind soon. It's only a matter of time now. I don't know about you but I'll kill him before my mother is pulled into his bullshit."

I lifted an eyebrow.

"She's already in his bullshit," I reminded him. "Or did you forget how you got here?"

"Feel how you feel but I'm still here giving you information I could keep close to the chest if I wanted."

I had no argument for that.

"Was that everything?"

He nodded but made no move to leave.

"I need to ask you something," he said, shaking his head.

"Never mind. I'll let you know when I learn anything else. You should warn your mother not to sign any documents he hands over without reading them first."

Something about the look in his eyes made me grab his arm before he moved past me completely.

"Ask your question."

I released him and we faced one another.

He looked to be working himself up to it and I knew before he got it out what it would be.

"Yeah," I said, deciding to save him from the inner battle he was having with the answer he'd been looking for.

Understanding passed between us and all the animosity I'd held toward him evaporated.

He nodded and started toward the door he'd come in from.

"Aye, Harlem."

He halted his strides but didn't turn around.

"If you ever need to talk…"

"Yeah," he replied, opening the door. "Same goes for you."

As he disappeared on the other side, my stomach twisted.

I guess we were one in the same.

With the information he laid out, I went to see my mother at the townhome she and my father used as a second home. It was closer to his work but their full-time residence was in Maryland—a home I hadn't been to in a long time.

I still really wasn't fucking with her but I also cared enough to warn her.

"You're just in time for lunch," she said after letting me inside. "Mona made chicken tortilla soup and sandwiches."

"Not hungry," I replied, following her into the kitchen.

She turned and regarded me closely.

"Ricardo, if you're here to make me feel bad about our conversation the last time—"

I waved her off; we had bigger shit to discuss.

"I need to ask you something and it's imperative that you're honest."

She busied herself making two portions of food, even after I'd said I wasn't hungry.

"I'm listening..."

"Did Aunt Lina give a baby up for adoption?" I asked, getting straight to the first thing we needed to discuss.

If anyone knew the truth it would be my mother.

She halted her movements but didn't lift her gaze to meet mine.

"Not to my knowledge," she lied, resuming her task.

"Try again but this time don't lie to me."

"Ricardo, why are you asking this? What does it matter if she did or didn't?"

I rested my elbows on the counter and stared at her, waiting for an answer that didn't come in the form of another question.

"Some things need to stay buried and this is one of them," she said, confirming without actually saying it.

It was good enough for me.

"Did you know she left a will behind?"

This time she looked up, her brows pinched together in confusion.

"Where did you get that information? There was no will. Your father made a big deal about her being irresponsible and having to settle her matters even after death."

Hmm, I hummed.

"Doesn't matter..." I waved it off. "There's something else we need to talk about."

She set a plate in front of me and I pushed it away.

"I can't eat that."

"Why are you always so difficult, Ricardo? I'm trying to

have a quick meal with my son who showed up unannounced, might I add."

"I don't know, maybe my allergy to tomatoes is the reason."

It was a shame how much my own mother didn't know about me, but I never expected more from her or my father. They were always about themselves.

Had Mona--the longtime cook for the family--still been here, she would've stepped in immediately with another meal for me. The staff I'd grown up with knew my sisters and me better than our parents ever could.

"Oh..." She took the plate away. "I forgot about that."

"As for showing up unannounced, did you not do the same recently? Let's be reasonable here."

She ignored me and started rummaging through a drawer.

My mother had aged tremendously it seemed. The grey's in her hair were more prominent. She looked stressed, worn down.

I straightened and got to the point.

"Did you know he's being investigated for judicial misconduct?"

"Who are you talking about?"

I sighed.

"Who else? Stop pretending like you don't know and help me understand why I had to hear it from my half-brother."

Her eyes widened and then went cold.

"Ricardo Carter, don't talk to me like I'm one of your—"

"One of my what? Go ahead and say it, tell me how you really feel about me."

She scoffed and waved her dainty fingers at me.

"Why must you take everything to heart? You're my son and I love you."

I hated that having feelings about any fucking thing in this family meant you were trippin' or being sensitive, when it was bigger than that and always had been.

"I take it to heart because I have a right to. My feelings are mine and they fucking matter. Why is that so hard for you to see? He's playing you and you're so far gone that you don't see it."

She shook her head, still in denial.

"You don't know what you're talking about and *my marriage* isn't up for discussion."

I chuckled.

"Your marriage is for image purposes. If you meant anything to him at all, there wouldn't be another grown ass man out there that looks just like me. If you mattered to him he wouldn't be fucking his chief of staff right under your nose, Ma."

The glass she'd been holding came flying at me and I ducked out the way.

As it shattered, she screamed for me to leave but I refused.

She would hear what I had to say and then I'd be done with it.

"Why are you doing this?" she questioned through tears. "Why are you hurting me when I'm already broken? Can't you see it?"

I could never tell if she was being sincere or trying to manipulate me.

"Look at me and tell me if you see that I'm broken too. He broke me a long time ago but I made a choice to get away from it."

"Your father loves you—"

"For fucks sake!" I bellowed, silencing her. "What kind of father abuses his son?"

She rushed forward, throwing her fists at my chest in a fit of rage.

What should have hurt left me numb inside and out.

"Don't you dare slander your father's name. He never laid a finger on you, I would know!"

"Right..." I took a step back and nodded. "I never expected you to believe me, let alone protect me. You slept in a bed with a man who let grown women touch his son while he watched. He's a sick son of a bitch."

I turned toward the door, tired of fighting with a lost cause.

"Don't sign anything he gives you without reading it if you want to stay out of jail, but what the fuck do I know."

I left feeling defeated.

It sucked not being believed.

CHAPTER 17
GAIA

Pierson's files were taking me on a journey.

Had he seen his demise coming?

I'd been so worried about Rocco that our reason for being in D.C. slipped my mind.

It was only when I walked past the bag sitting at the end of the sofa in the family room that I was reminded of the task at hand.

With my favorite energy drink in hand, I spread the papers out on the kitchen island and worked through them one by one.

He'd saved everything from the last two years--receipts, banks statements, and offshore account numbers were only a few of the things he kept locked up in that safe.

Everything needed to expose a conniving man but nothing concrete to help answer questions about Angelo, if it was connected at all.

I pulled my laptop in front of me and opened a secure server.

There were enough breadcrumbs in his footnotes to get the

ball rolling on what I needed to do next. With the Kellen and Beck employee homepage up, I used a mirror login to get into the system.

It would read as a normal login from inside the building, and unless they had someone on their staff better than me, no one would know the difference.

Once inside, I searched for their digital files on Robert and started to compare them to the ones Pierson had in his home.

The deposits coming in looked to be above board but three stood out.

I clicked through each and eyed the footnotes.

Each read the same: *deposit from the estate of Alina Carter.*

"That's odd," I mumbled, moving around the island to find the ledger book Pierson kept.

Flipping through it slowly, I found identical deposits that were labeled as from Lina's estate. Next to each were the same account numbers to an offshore account in Switzerland.

It didn't surprise me that he'd moved the money but what did were the dates.

Rocco had said his aunt died five years ago but the deposits were made seven years ago.

I went searching for the will next and flipped through for the name of the lawyer that had drawn it up.

Danielle Schwartz of Barron, Rosenberg and Associates.

I googled the company but found no profile for an attorney by that name.

Gulping the rest of my energy drink down, I got to work looking for the woman and without much effort I found her.

The daughter of David Barron, name partner at Barron, Rosenberg, and associates.

"Did he..."

I searched her name in D.C bar directory and laughed.

"That sneaky muthafucka," I mused after finding that

she'd been disbarred for forging and falsifying documents a year ago.

It's a fake.

He faked his sister's will to get the money from her estate and then moved it after Danielle was indicted on a slew of charges.

How the fuck is he getting away with this?

And what did Valarie Stokes have to do with it; if Lina had a will that's hidden somewhere, why did Valarie still get money?

Was she in on the scheme?

The connections Robert Carter needed to pull something off like this were deep and while I was good at what I did, this was becoming bigger than me.

With nowhere left to turn, I decided to call Rocco.

"Yeah," he answered, his voice barely above a whisper.

What I'd called for went out the window upon hearing the sadness seeping through the phone.

"What's wrong?"

He was silent for a long while.

"Met with my mom, didn't go well."

"Do you... Do you want to talk about it?"

"What did you need?" he asked, ignoring my question.

I listened for noise in the background but got nothing.

"Where are you?"

"The garage," he answered without avoiding.

I hung up and slipped my feet into a pair of Nike slides, heading straight for the elevator next.

With Caution, I approached the car he'd driven today and opened the passenger door.

He didn't turn to acknowledge me as I slid inside but took my hand and laced our fingers.

I rested my head on his arm and we sat in silence together.

"I'm not sure I can have her in my life anymore," he said after a while. "I've held on for too long."

"You have to do what's best for you, even if it hurts. And no matter what, I got your back."

It didn't matter why or what had transpired for him to come to this decision.

"You mean that?" he asked, lifting my head with his free hand.

"I mean it," I affirmed, caressing the side of his face. "You deserve to have peace. And being states away shouldn't be how you acquire it. This is your home, right?"

He licked his lips and nodded.

"I know it's where you'd rather be," I went on. "Setting boundaries with the people who mean you no good is a start."

"What if I asked you to be here with me? Would it be selfish of me to take you away from your family?"

I shook my head.

"Being a few hours away from my family doesn't scare me. I can see them whenever I want, by plane or car."

"Does that mean you'd consider making my home yours?"

"Ricardo, I want to be with you whether it's in Philly or Jersey or right here in D.C."

He sighed and looked away.

"Maybe I should build something in between the three. Find another sleepy town like Blackthorne or Grayfall and make it ours."

Ours.

He wanted us to have something for just the two of us and I found myself wanting the same after the idea had been planted.

"Do you want to talk about what happened with your mom?" I asked, deciding to try my luck with the understanding that he could say no.

The silence that followed went on for a while and it unnerved me.

"We don't have to. Come inside and—"

"I went to see her after meeting with Harlem. My intentions were to talk about Lina and warn her about what Harlem said but shit went left."

I'd forgotten that he'd left to meet with his brother.

"What did Harlem say?"

"Robert is being investigated for judicial misconduct. It's been under wraps for the last year."

Did Harlem really have the kind of connections that would award him the luxury of having that kind of information? He seemed smart and calculated but I couldn't judge him fairly just from that one encounter we had.

"While I was going through Pierson's files I found something," I revealed. "You said your aunt died five years ago but your father received three payments from her estate two years before that. They add up to what was left to him in her will."

He released my hand and brushed it down his face.

"I think the will is a fake to cover his tracks, from what? I don't know but the lawyer, Danielle Schwartz, was disbarred and indicted a year ago. Now that I know what you do, it sounds like she gave him up and that's when the investigation started against him."

"She lied about having any knowledge of an adoption," he said, leaning back in his seat. "I'm almost positive she told the truth when I asked her about a will. She was adamant that my father had made a fuss about having to clean up Lina's affairs again."

"You know..." I tapped the dashboard as something occurred to me. "I don't think Angelo is her son. Wouldn't he be too young?"

He was only fifty-five.

Rocco glanced at me with a frown marring his handsome face.

"I didn't think of that," he said. "My dad is ten years older than him, sometimes I forget that Lina was younger than him too. He and my mom started having children late, right when his career started to take off."

"Whoa..." I envisioned his face again. "I wouldn't have guessed that."

Rocco hummed.

"There's only one person we can get answers from," he said. "Think you can find Valarie Stokes?"

I lifted an eyebrow, offended that he even had to ask.

"My bad, Shortcake..." He smiled, brightening his face a little. "I know you can do it."

I nodded, choosing not to give him a hard time. His smile was worth it.

"Should we go inside?" I asked. "Or..."

I wasn't sure how to take the conversation back, now that he'd climb his way out of the dark hole his mind had been in. Even though I wanted to know what happened with his mom to put him in such a bad place, I couldn't chance dragging him down again.

It wasn't worth it.

"I want to confide in you but not with this looming over us," he said, almost as if he'd read my mind. "Let's find the answers we need and be done with it. Then, we'll talk, alright?"

I nodded and leaned over the console, pulling him toward me by his shirt.

As our lips met in the gentlest kiss we'd shared thus far, my promise to protect him intensified.

Everybody could see me about Ricardo Carter, including his parents.

193

Especially them.

I got to work after we went inside, going with a simpler plan to get Valerie's attention.

A quick search produced her last known phone number but no address.

I grabbed my phone and connected it to my computer. After loading my tracking software, I dialed the number and placed my phone on speaker as Rocco walked in.

He'd changed into a pair of sweats and long sleeved t-shirt, both black.

I liked how black looked on him and found myself admiring his frame longer than I'd meant to.

"Hello," a voice greeted, prompting my software to begin its search.

I looked away from Rocco and focused on the task at hand.

"Hi," I spoke back. "I'm looking for a Valerie Stokes."

The line went quiet for a long while and I knew it was her.

"This is Valerie and who am I speaking with?"

"My name is Stephanie Delaney and I was hired by an Angelo Bianchi to find his biological family. Recently I came across some documents with your name as the social worker on his case. I'm having a problem and was hoping you could clarify some things for me."

"I'm sorry, I can't help," she responded quickly. "If it were me who facilitated the adoption then it's closed and sealed by law. Your best option is to petition the court to unseal the records."

I sighed, pretending to be disappointed.

"I see. Maybe you can help with something else instead. Is it okay if I ask you a couple of questions. You can answer yes or no, if possible."

"Again, I'm not sure I can help but go ahead."

I glanced at my computer screen.

"Can you hold while I grab a pen?"

She huffed a little but that didn't matter to me. As long as I kept her on the phone for three minutes, I'll know her exact location.

"Sure but we need to make this quick."

"Thank you," I said, placing her on mute.

"What are you doing, Shortcake?" Rocco asked as he stepped closer.

"Tracking her."

He leaned over my shoulder to get a better look.

"Such a criminal," he mused before kissing my cheek and walking around to the other side of the island.

I waited until her location populated and unmuted the phone.

"Hi, sorry, Valerie. Just one question. Does the name Alina Carter mean anything to you?"

She gasped and then the line went dead right after.

"Definitely her," Rocco and I said at once.

I clicked the red pin on the map and zoomed in to see that it was indeed a residential area.

With an address to work with, I searched for the deed in the District of Columbia property records.

The search came back to a corporation, whose name I'd seen before.

"If this is the home she's living in, then she's working with your father in some capacity."

I brought the laptop to where he stood and then shuffled through the papers I'd left lying around.

"Here..." I handed him the document in question. "This was in Pierson's file and that's the name on the deed."

He looked at both and then turned his attention to me.

"I need to know how many adoptions she's facilitated over the years. Give me a moment to get in touch with my contact and in the meantime I'll track her just in case she moves locations. That call might've spooked her."

He hummed.

"Do you think it spooked her enough to call my father?"

I nodded.

"I'm sure it did."

Rocco nodded and shut my laptop.

"Waiting for your contact might fuck up this lead. If my father thinks we're on to him, she'll disappear before we ever get answers. Let's go now before it's too late."

I nodded and looked down at my feet.

"Let me grab my gun and sneakers and then we can go."

Twenty minutes later, we pulled into what looked to be a quiet Columbia Heights neighborhood.

The sun had just set and there was no movement outside the row homes on both sides of the street. Rocco found a spot to park a few houses down from Valarie's and turned to me.

"She'll know my face and I don't want my presence to spook her more than she probably already is. You knock and I'll stand on the sidewalk in front of the house next door to avoid cameras, if any."

I nodded and we got out, both checking our surroundings before executing his plan.

Halfway up the steps leading to the door, I noticed a camera just above the door and looked into it for a short moment in case she was watching.

Get a good look at my face.

After another second or two, I knocked and then rang the doorbell.

It wasn't long before the door open, only a fraction of the way and a pair of blue-green eyes appeared.

"Yes?" she murmured, almost as if she didn't want anyone to hear her.

"Hi, are you Valarie?"

She looked me up and down and then widened it a little more.

"Did Robert send you?" she asked, revealing her tiny frame.

She was high yellow with dark hair that was streaked grey.

"No, sorry. We talked on the phone not long ago and—"

Her eyes widened before she slammed the door shut.

"Go away or I'll call the police!" she threatened from the other side. "How did you find my address?"

"Do you want me to leave or tell you how I found your address?" I queried.

When I was met with silence, I tried again.

"Valarie, I know it's probably scary me showing up here like this. But I think we both know that it's probably best you talk to me. Whatever security Robert is offering you, it won't last long when he's in jail."

Almost immediately, I heard the locks disengage.

"Jail?" she questioned, opening the door but keeping the screen door shut. "What do you mean?"

"He's being investigated for judicial misconduct and he's very dangerous. Let me help you."

She looked conflicted and I knew it would take more than my word for her to believe me.

I looked over my shoulder and waved for Rocco to make his appearance.

"Who—oh!"

Her eyes bucked at the sight of him.

"Valerie," Rocco greeted, his tone not so inviting but at least he'd tried. "It's been a long time."

She unlocked the screen door and stepped out.

"It's been a very long time."

He nodded and moved to stand beside me.

"I know this isn't ideal but we have some questions and I think you could help."

She looked between us and nodded.

"Sure, come in but your father can't know about this."

Rocco and I glanced at one another and followed her inside.

Jackpot.

CHAPTER 18
ROCCO

Valarie led us into a family room and waved for us to sit on the love seat across from her reclining chair.

"Sorry for the mess," she said, looking around as if to see it from our eyes. "I know it's not what you might be used to."

Her eyes were on me as she spoke.

The place was sparsely decorated but still homey; it wasn't messy as she claimed it to be either.

"We don't care about that," Gaia said, waving her off. "Ricardo and I are only here to understand some of the things we found recently."

Valarie nodded and took a seat.

She looked nervous, her gaze moving between us and around the room over and over.

"Did you call my father?" I asked, watching her fidget at the mention of him.

She shook her head and looked down at her clasped hands.

"I wanted to but changed my mind and then you two showed up."

"That's good, Valarie," Gaia told her. "I'm sorry we accosted you this way."

"It's okay. When I heard Alina's name I couldn't believe it. Five years was so long ago. Losing her was hard for me."

Gaia nodded and I sat back, deciding it was best she did the talking.

My way of getting information out of someone wouldn't be useful here.

"Why did she leave you money in her will?" Gaia asked, leaning forward with her elbows on her knees.

Valarie wouldn't make eye contact and I didn't trust a soul who couldn't look into the eyes of the person they were talking to.

"I'm still not sure why," she murmured, sticking with the lie.

Gaia glanced at me and I nodded.

"We know the will is a fake, Valarie. It's best if you're honest with us."

She looked up, surprised.

"I... I didn't know it was fake at first," she admitted, shaking her head. "But by the time I'd accepted the money, there was no turning back. Robert is not the kind of man you betray."

"Why did he offer you the money?"

She stared at Gaia for what felt like forever before responding.

"Valarie wanted it to go to her..." She looked away. "I had only just started working at the adoption agency my mother also worked at when Lina learned she was pregnant. We were fresh out of college and her parents were strict and very religious. She wanted to have a plan in motion before telling them."

I could never imagine my grandparents as strict but I guess

it's true that when your children have children you lose some of the bite you had with your own.

"And adoption was the plan?"

"It hadn't been at first but then she showed up one day, her mind made up, and there wasn't anything I could do to convince her otherwise. Eventually, she told her parents and they were oddly upset about it. They offered to raise the kid but she refused and started the process around the 6 month mark."

Gaia sat back and nodded.

"Was it a boy or a girl?"

Valarie smiled a little.

"A girl," she said, confirming Angelo not being Lina's son. "She gave her up without a second glance and never looked back. At least at first. Years passed and she was doing bad; I think regret was eating at her because suddenly she wanted to meet her daughter—to make amends. She started the process of reaching out and then she died of an overdose."

"Did you find her death suspicious?" I asked, losing the battle to stay quiet.

"Not necessarily. She was using a lot to cope but when I learned that her fortune had gone to Robert, I knew something wasn't right. By then, he'd implicated me and I couldn't risk losing everything."

It was selfish of her but I understood.

When your livelihood was on the line you'll do anything to protect it. For her it was about survival. I personally could never betray someone I love and cherish to save myself but everybody wasn't built like me.

My eyes shifted to Gaia as she began to speak.

She was built like me though and as loyal as they come.

"You said before that she wanted her money to go where exactly?" Gaia asked, taking over the questioning again.

"I hadn't been sure if she meant it at the time but she'd mentioned briefly wanting to leave everything to her daughter. She told me that it was the least she could do."

"I was under the impression that my grandparents hadn't left her any money."

Valarie frowned and shook her head.

"They split the estate between Robert and her, both left with an equal about of money and assets."

Mmm, I hummed.

My grandparents passed a month apart ten years ago. When their wills were read it wasn't done in a group setting. Instead, we each sat with the lawyer one by one and had a private reading of only what was meant for that person to hear.

At the time, I hadn't thought anything of it but now it seemed they'd done it to avoid disputes. My father had talked openly about being left everything and Lina had pretended that it was true.

Was that his motive all along? *Money.*

"There's something you should know," Valarie said, pulling me from my thoughts.

Our eyes met and I nodded.

"Your father and aunt had a big fight right before she died. I vividly remember her calling me distraught but she wouldn't tell me what the fight was about. Then, she said something that stuck with me all these years, haunted to me really."

She pushed up from the chair and walked over to the window.

"She said, clear as day, '*He did this to me and I've suffered every day since*'..." Valarie turned and looked at me, her eyes filled with deep sadness. "'*How could he hurt me this way when I've only ever loved him?*' She ended the call after that and the next day she was found dead in her bathroom."

Gaia gasped but I couldn't fathom what Valarie was trying to convey.

My father was a sick man but...

I shook my head.

"I have to get out of here," she said suddenly. "I've lived in fear for a long time. Afraid of what he'd do to me if I skipped town and never looked back but I can't do this anymore."

"We can help you," Gaia offered as she stood. "I have a few connections in the city that can take you in and move you around until there's a safer way to get you out of town, but you have to pack as light as you can and go with us no—"

The window shattered and I reached for Gaia, dragging her into my lap as a bullet pierced the back of Valarie's head and she dropped.

"Fuck!" I cursed, checking Gaia for injury.

My mind wouldn't work until I knew for sure that she hadn't been touched.

"I'm fine..."

She pushed my hands away and got down on the floor. Lying flat on her belly, she checked Valarie for a pulse.

"This is bad," she said as I scaled the wall to get to the window. "She's dead. I wasn't finished asking her questions."

I knew who ever sent the shot had only intended on killing Valarie and was long gone.

A professional, who used a silencer.

There hadn't been the tale-tale *pop* that lingered in the air after squeezing the trigger.

"The cameras," I said, shaking my head. "Either he knows we're here or she lied about not calling him."

"She asked if Robert sent me after answering the door but I didn't think anything of it." She shook her head. "We have to leave her," she decided as she stood with her phone in hand.

"I'll make a call to a friend and have them remotely access the security system."

While she talked in code on the phone, mine rang and before I pulled it from my pocket I knew who it was.

"That's a sticky situation you're dealing with right now," my father mused.

I chuckled but chose not to respond.

"I can make it all disappear like it never happened, Ricardo. All you have to do is ask."

I glanced at Gaia who was watching me closely.

Looking into her eyes, I made a choice that would probably take me away from her but the people I loved would be safe from harm.

She would be safe.

"And what would I have to do in exchange for your help?" I asked, playing along with no intention of needing it.

"Meet me in an hour at our old spot. Leave there right now and don't touch anything else."

He ended the call and I sent a text to a contact that'll clear the place to my liking.

"Let's go."

I took Gaia's hand and she pulled it away, forcing me to look at her.

"What did he say?"

"He wants to meet in exchange for his help."

"We don't need his help," she argued. "I can have this cleared up in no time."

I led her out of the family room and toward the front door.

My father knew I didn't need his help but he offered it because there was something else he wanted from me.

"I know but some shit can't be fixed when the root of the problem is still living and breathing amongst us."

She dug the heel of her sneaker into the floor to stop me from walking.

I dropped her hand and spun around, snatching Gaia into me.

She was frustrating and stubborn and I loved her.

"I know what you're thinking," she stated calmly, her eyes trying to find reason in mine. "But, you can't, Ricardo. He's the goddam attorney general. I can't let you do it, not like this."

I knew she was right but what other choice did I have?

"Sometimes violence is the only answer," I said, pressing my lips to her forehead. "Even when your father is the attorney general."

Robert Carter was a menace to society who needed to be put down like a rabid dog.

And I was the only person who could do it.

Much to her dismay, I dropped Gaia off at home and went to meet my father.

Our *old spot* wasn't anywhere special, just an old warehouse that had been converted into an afterhours spot. It was where men with high powered jobs went to play or hang with the luxury of discretion.

No cameras.

I hadn't stepped foot inside in almost ten years but nothing had changed.

It still had that same stale liquor and cigarette smell.

My skin chilled as memories from my childhood came flooding back. I brushed my fingers down my arms to relieve myself of the goosebumps, but the shit that happened to me here could never be pushed away.

I moved through the warehouse—noticing that he had been cleared out, which meant my father wanted the privacy. Little did he know, it worked in my favor.

Toward the back were a few private rooms blocked off with thick velvet curtains and I entered the one at the very end.

My father sat with one leg propped up on the table, a cigar in his mouth, and a glass filled with an amber liquid. If he still had the same tastes then it was three fingers Macallan, chilled.

"Have a seat, Son."

He dropped his foot from the table and sat up straight.

"Let's make a deal," he went on, eyes meeting mine as I sat across from him.

"You need to tell me a few things first," I said, leaning back. "Start with why you had Valarie killed?"

He scoffed.

"She took the money I offered, not because she thought it came from your aunt, but because she'd already been stealing from her for me..." He chuckled. "Her job was to take small amounts at a time and they added up after a while."

He shrugged.

"That doesn't answer my question."

He sipped from his glass and I held his gaze while he took his sweet time.

We could sit here all day, I had the patience of a saint.

"She had to die because of you," he said, lips curling into a smile. "Had you and your *fiancée* not sought her out she'd still be alive and well."

I shrugged.

Valarie had been collateral damage and I could live with that.

"I'll take everything she said as true."

"Did she happen to mention how in love she was with me? How she betrayed her best friend by stealing money on my behalf and helped me fake her will by hiring Danielle Schwartz? Or did she leave those details out?"

He laughed but it quickly turned into anger.

His fist hit the table so hard it knocked his drink over onto the floor, shattering the glass it'd been in.

What a waste of good whiskey, I thought.

I regarded him nonchalantly without so much as a flinch.

"You don't get to question me!" he roared, revealing his true self.

"You should work on your anger," I suggested. "It's unbecoming of you, throwing temper tantrums at your big age..." I leaned forward and rested my elbows on the table. "We're here to make a deal, so let's make a deal."

He schooled his anger but I knew he was simmering, and it felt good to piss him off.

"Being this confident when you left your woman unprotected isn't smart, Ricardo."

The threat didn't move me and I visibly watched his mask falter, only for a second, but it was there.

"If you send men after her they won't leave alive," I said, waving my hand. "Gaia isn't a damsel in distress who needs to be saved from the big bad wolf, she can handle her own. Though for your sake, it might be best you call off your dogs. If she's touched, or a piece of hair is out of place, or a drop of sweat is on her skin from anything other than running her laps at the track, I won't be able to stop the full force of the mafia coming for you. And *Dad,* I promise I'll let them tear you limb from limb after I get my turn."

He'd underestimated her worth, but I hadn't expected anything less from a man who used and abused everybody he encountered.

"You take my words too seriously, Son. I see you still haven't learned to take a joke."

I laughed, slapping the table dramatically.

"Ha. Ha. Ha. How funny of you, Robert the fucking comedian. You should take this act on the road."

From the look in his eyes, it was only a matter of time before he broke.

My father never liked my sharp tongue.

By the time I'd shot up in height and size, we were going toe to toe in fist fights.

I wanted to knock the fake smug smirk off his face.

"Her daughter was yours, wasn't she?" I asked, tipping my head.

His eyes grew cold and the smirk disappeared.

"How dare you slander my name!" he shouted, not helping his case in any way.

"Someone's angry," I muttered. "If it isn't the truth, just say it. No need to yell."

He jumped up, still quick and limber for his age, and knocked over his chair.

The table between us went flying and he charged me, answering my question without saying a fucking word. I lifted my boot clad foot and kicked him in the chest, sending him flying into the wall without much effort.

Slowly, I stood with my gun drawn but didn't approach.

I was man enough to give him time to recover before I put a bullet in his head and called it a day.

"You can't kill me," he said, rising with his fingers gripping his chest. "We both know, you can't."

"Robert, you don't know me at all. I've taken lives for less. Your status is the least of my worries."

I put my gun to his head and for the first time I saw fear in my father's cold dark eyes.

He feared me, the man he'd turned me into.

"You were so confident I'd bend to your will that you came here without back up or a weapon. How dumb can you be?"

He blinked and the fear washed away, leaving only the conniving man I've known my entire life.

"What do you want?" he asked, ready to make a deal. "You want the truth about your aunt, is that it? I'm a monster to you but to her I was a goddamn king!"

There was this faraway look in his eyes I'd never seen before, a sadness.

"She was the only woman I'd ever loved and we couldn't be together."

I frowned, sick to my stomach by his confession.

"What the fuck. She was your sister!"

How deranged could one be to sleep with their own flesh and blood?

"Shut the fuck up!" he yelled, stumbling backward. "You know nothing! She was my best friend. The love of my life and not my goddamn sister. Your grandfather insisted on taking her in after his sister gave birth to twins, a boy and a girl. She didn't want them."

He'd said the shit as if her being his cousin made their weird ass relationship better.

"I remember it vividly," he went on, seemingly lost in the story. "They used Victoria's mother to facilitate the adoptions. The boy went to another family, someone your grandfather knew."

I almost didn't believe him but the look in his eyes, the pain, it was real.

He was telling the truth.

"And you got her pregnant?" I asked.

"It was an accident," he confessed. "I'd just met your mother and she was upset about it. We crossed a line, I promised I'd never cross again. The only choice we had was to get rid of it but she insisted on adoption, wanting a part of us out there living and breathing. I hated her for it, for putting me through that."

"And that's where Valarie came into play?"

He nodded.

"Her mother was dead by then and she was the next best option for a discrete under the table adoption. Ricardo, I know you see me as a monster and maybe I am, but I loved her and I didn't hurt her. At least in the way you think. I never laid a hand on Lina, it was—"

A shot rang out and for the second time today, I saw a body drop.

My father's eyes were wide and blood pooled from his head. The curtains shifted and I couldn't believe who I was seeing.

You've got to be kidding me.

CHAPTER 19
GAIA

I paced.

It was the only thing keeping me from tracking his phone.

Such a stupid man, I thought.

A beautifully complicated but stupid man.

I checked my watch and an hour had already passed since he dropped me at home.

I'd never in my life felt so useless.

Ugh!

On the verge of screaming and breaking some shit to feel better, my phone rang and brought me back from the brink of destruction.

I snatched it off the sofa and eyed Luci's name.

Ignoring her call, I decided to make my own moves.

If Rocco wanted his father dead, then I would help him execute it.

Grabbing my laptop, I opened my tracking software and typed his phone number in.

There was an encryption installed to block my access and it

took a second to break through but I got in and pinned his location.

My phone rang again and I sighed, picking up Lucia's call this time.

"Luci, I can't talk right now."

"What's wrong? I hear it in your voice, so don't lie to me."

"Rocco is about to do something stupid and I'm going to help him," I confessed, writing the address down and closing my laptop. "I need to call you back but maybe be on standby in case shit hits the fan. He'll need a lawyer. Not just any lawyer, he'll need Luca."

I could hear her moving around as I stepped into my boots and zipped them up.

"I can be there in—"

"No!" I shouted, cutting her off. "Do not come here unless I call for you, Lucia. It's important that you stay where you are, far away from this. Alright?"

She was silent for too long and because I knew my cousin, she was more than likely contemplating on if she wanted to listen or not.

Stubborn ass Moretti woman.

"Can't believe this shit," she mumbled. "Nobody wants me to have any fun. Not you or Violet."

I had no idea what she meant by that, nor did I have the time to ask.

"Just sit tight for me."

I hung up and left my phone behind, taking my encrypted burner in its place.

Grabbing the keys to his blacked out Escalade, I stepped into the garage as the door lifted and the same impala we'd been in with Manny pulled in.

The man himself, rolled the window down and said, "Get in."

"Did he send you?" I asked, sliding into the passenger seat.

"My only job is to deliver you to him safe and sound."

I bit my lip and stared out the window as he drove us to a desolate part of town.

Every few miles there was a business or a warehouse but then nothing.

"You care for him, right?"

I kept my gaze on the emptiness staring back at me.

"I love him," I confessed.

"Glad to hear that. Don't fail him, Gaia."

Goodness, Ricardo.

What have you gotten yourself into?

It felt like an eternity but in reality hadn't taken long for Manny to get us to our destination--an old warehouse that looked to be converted into a venue or club.

I wasn't sure until we went inside and I saw the bar against the wall and raggedy tables and chairs strewn about.

"This way," Manny directed, leading us through the deserted space toward a back hallway.

I spotted Rocco standing outside of a room blocked with a black velvet curtain talking to Wyatt right away. Relieved that he was safe and unharmed, I rushed him, knocking us both into the wall.

"Don't ever leave me behind again," I snapped, wrapping my fingers around his loose locs. "Never. We are a team from now on, got it?"

Our eyes danced for a short time, emotions high but real as fuck.

He nodded eventually and kissed my forehead.

"I got it, Shortcake," he murmured against my skin.

"This is cute and all but Gaia we need to wipe the security system," Wyatt said. "This place isn't supposed to have cameras but we found a room with monitors."

I turned and eyed the not so carefree man I'd met on New Year's Eve.

He wasn't celebrating anymore and before me was the head of a crime family—a man about his business.

I nodded.

"Show me what I'm covering up."

Wyatt looked at Rocco over my head and then waved for me to enter.

I flipped the curtain back and there was Robert, laying on his side in a pool of blood.

But the person sitting near the body, I hadn't expected to see.

"Why is she here?" I asked, eyeing a despondent Deidre.

Rocco's mother stared off into space, not once acknowledging my presence.

She was in shock.

"She followed him here and overheard our conversation," Rocco explained. "Killed him before I ever got the chance."

What the fuck?

I spun around to face him, shocked by the revelation.

"What did he say that set her off?"

Rocco sighed.

"Confessed his undying love for his sister, who apparently wasn't his actual sister."

It all suddenly made sense.

"The baby..."

"It was his," he confirmed. "I thought he killed Lina for her money but I don't think so now. He was in the middle of saying something when she shot him."

My mind was working in overdrive, something about this wasn't right. His mother showing up here with a gun felt much more calculated than a woman simply following her husband for answers.

"You said she knew about the adoption and lied, right?"

He nodded.

"Step out and let me talk to her."

He looked conflicted but I wasn't taking no for an answer.

Eventually, he agreed and they cleared room.

Taking a breath, I turned and walked over to Deirdre.

As I dropped into a squat in front of her, she met my gaze.

"Why did you follow him here?" I asked.

She barely blinked.

"You know what I think?" I went on. "I think you were hoping to catch him with another woman. Is that it?"

I was met with nothing but silence.

"Or maybe for once you decided to believe your son and came to see if he was setting you up. Is that it?"

She flinched and I had part of my answer.

"Instead, he confessed to loving someone else but you knew that already, didn't you?"

The haze seemed to clear and she spoke.

"You don't know anything."

I chuckled.

"I know that you're a sorry excuse for a mother," I murmured for only her to hear. "And now here you are, allowing your son to clean up your mess—a mess that was created well before today."

"My son—"

"Is not a pawn. He's not yours to use as you please and then toss away when you feel like it..." I leaned in closer, my lips close to her ear. "You should be dead, too."

She gasped and slid back, her body bumping Robert's corpse.

At the realization of what was lying beside her, she screamed and jumped up.

"How dare you!" she yelled, turning her anger on me just as I wanted.

I stood and shrugged.

There was no need to glance behind me, I knew Rocco, Wyatt, and Manny had entered.

"You have no right to be here," she ranted.

"But I'm here to help clean up your mess and trust when I say that you need me."

"Ricardo, how can you let her disrespect me like—"

"You're lucky I don't do more than disrespect you after the way you talked to me before..." I stepped toward her and she backed away. "It was you, wasn't it? You killed Lina and made it look like an overdose, didn't you?"

It all made sense now.

She was equally as bad as her dead husband.

"You can't—"

"Quit with the bullshit, Deidre. You wanted him to yourself and killed her, didn't you!"

I'd backed her into a corner.

Ricardo wouldn't step in and she had to know that by now.

My line of questioning was too spot on for him to save her from it.

"Just admit it," I said softly. "You thought he would love you more when she was gone but instead he sought peace in other women. He never loved you, even after you gave him children to use and abuse as he pleased. That makes you the worst kind of human being."

"He was mine!" she screamed, finally admitting it. "But he was hers, too. And there couldn't be two of us. I did what I needed to do."

"You never cease to amaze me," Rocco said, sounding so goddamn disappointed.

I hated that this was the outcome, that once again he was

hurt by the actions of the people who were supposed to be his family.

She tried to get past me and I wasn't having it.

"I promised your son that I'd protect him..." I shook my head, coming to a decision that would either make or break my relationship with Rocco. "I see it now, clear as day. You are who he needs to be protected from."

I pulled my gun and secured it in my least dominate hand before she could blink, pressing it under her chin and pulling the trigger.

The sound was deafening but I heard the curses from behind me.

My ears rung and my skin was sticky from her blood and pieces of skull but it had to be done.

She had to go.

It was the only way he'd ever be happy, the only way to grant him the peace he deserved.

I stumbled back and into a pair of arms I knew belonged to Rocco. He turned me to face him and I couldn't look into his eyes.

"Give me the gun, baby," he said softly, not an ounce of anger in his cadence.

I released it and he handed it to Manny.

Wyatt handed him a towel and he started to wipe me down.

"Give us a minute."

They left and I broke down.

"I'm sorry," I cried, holding onto him. "I... I had to do it. She didn't deserve you. She was going to break you and—"

He pulled me into his chest and silenced my pleas for him to understand.

"You're right," he muttered. "She had to go and I'm glad it was you who pulled the trigger and not me. Thank you, Gaia."

I couldn't believe what I was hearing.

He wasn't upset but thanking me.

"You—"

"We need to stage this," he cut in. "And I need you to wipe the security system. This is gonna take some work but we'll get through it and then we'll talk, okay?"

I nodded, still in disbelief.

"The security room is down the hall. Go there and I'll call my sisters. I can't keep this from them and we'll need their help."

He sounded so confident.

Would his sisters really help and not hate me for what I'd done?

Could it really all be that simple?

It couldn't be, right?

CHAPTER 20
ROCCO

Noise from the hall drew me away from Gaia and toward the security room's door.

"Sit tight, baby. I need to handle my sisters."

She was in shock but working efficiently to encrypt and then erase the footage.

"Wyatt, if you don't move, I promise to make your life a living hell and—"

"Ally," I called, taking their attention off Wyatt who was only doing what I asked.

Allyson and Marie rushed over, both tossing questions at me at once.

"What's going on?" They asked in unison.

"Why are you back in this place?" Ree questioned, taking my hand. "You shouldn't be here reliving the things that happened here."

I appreciated her concern but the past was the last thing on my mind.

"There's something I need to tell the both of you and I'm

not sure how you'll react but we need to work together first and then you can hate me."

They shared a look.

"What is it?" Ally asked. "It doesn't matter. We'll always have your back, just like you had ours growing up."

I nodded, hoping what she said was true.

Neither of them would ever know it was Gaia who killed our mother. I'll take their hatred for the both of us before I let her endure it.

"I met dad here," I explained calmly. "We talked about... a lot and I'll give those details later but mom came, heard the things he'd said and killed him before I could."

I received no reaction, just blank stares.

Our father had terrorized us our whole lives, losing him might not affect them but our mother, that could be a different story.

"And mom, where's she?" Marie asked, brushing her hair off her shoulder.

Instead of answering with words, I led them to the room where both bodies were.

Ally stepped in first and then Ree followed, both taking steps back after seeing what was there.

I waited for their screams or sadness or tears but nothing.

Were we so fucked up that none of this affected us in the way that it should?

How the fuck could that be?

"What's the plan?" Ally asked, pulling a hair tie off her wrist.

As she wrapped her hair, Marie approached the bodies.

"Murder-suicide is the best option," she suggested, monotoned. "Leave the bodies here with the blood. The tables being turned and glass on the floor makes it look like a fight ensued already."

Ally walked the perimeter of the room, her eyes moving rapidly over the mess.

"No more people in or out of this room but Marie and me..." She took her phone out and sent a text. "I want the floor dusted, not mopped, to remove shoe prints."

It was the first time I'd seen them in fixer mode.

"Ricardo!" Marie yelled to gain my attention. "Did you hear us? We need to bring our team in, do you trust us?"

I looked between the two of them.

"How are you so calm?" I asked, needing to know. "Both of our parents are dead and neither of you are reacting how I thought you would."

Ally snorted. "Good riddance," she mumbled. "Marie was our mom, Rocco. You and I both know it. Maybe I'll be sad later but right now, I don't feel anything."

"I still want to know what happened," Marie admitted. "But, whatever it is won't make me hate you. Not as much as I hated him, never that much."

I nodded.

"I trust you," I told them. "Bring your team in and I'll have Wyatt's guys pull out. The less people here, the better."

"Good..." Ally dropped into a squat and started to remove our mother's shoes. "Go give your directives and then leave this to us. We have a routine and will work better without you here."

I frowned.

"We have to tell a specific story--one that will match the information we put out there in the coming weeks," Marie elaborated. "Don't worry. We know what we're doing. You have your thing and we have ours."

I left them and met Wyatt in the front of the bar where he sat with the owner.

"Say it again," he ordered, forcing the man to repeat the story we'd given him.

The story we'd concocted was simple but it would be effective.

Because my father had refused a protective detail when not handling official business, there wasn't anyone watching his back like there should be.

He was a smart but stupid man, and he got what he deserved.

"That's enough," I commanded, waving the older man away.

Wyatt stood and turned to me.

"How'd it go? They good?"

I nodded.

"Better than I expected but who knows what will happen when the media gets wind of this."

He took a deep breath.

"I have my men checking businesses leading here for cameras. Most of them have illegal shit going on and are out here to be away from eyes and ears..." He shook his head. "This was the best place for it to happen."

He wasn't wrong, had it been anywhere else there was no telling what could've come of this.

"I need a favor, Wy."

"You've been asking for a lot of favors. In a minute you'll owe me your life."

I chuckled.

"Make things right with Ace and I'll set you up with Luca and Enzo."

He smirked.

"Don't worry about that. I've already started to play my cards, it's only a matter of time before he agrees to my truce."

Mmm, I hummed holding out a piece of paper with an address on it.

"Josephina's team just finished cleaning this address. They left a something in the backyard and I need you to grab it for me, only you can do it."

He was good slipping in and out of places undetected, same as Manny who was preoccupied with something else.

"I'm on it..." He took it and grabbed my wrist. "Go check on your girl. We got this."

Wyatt started toward the door and paused halfway there.

"She's special," he said over his shoulder. "Protect her the same way she's set on protecting you."

I found my way to Gaia after he left, slipping into the security room to find her staring off into space.

"You shouldn't beat yourself up on my behalf, Shortcake," I said, smiling as she jumped up and rushed to get to me.

"I... I don't feel bad and that's what I've been afraid of," she admitted, staring up at me as if I had all the answers. "I should've let you handle it but she made me so angry and I couldn't stop myself."

Her skin was dotted with dried blood and if I searched hard enough, I knew I'd find pieces of my mother hidden in her hair and dark clothing, but she was still the most beautiful woman I'd ever encountered.

"Would you believe me if I said I knew what you were going to do before you did it?"

And I hadn't stopped her because part of me, a big part of me, wanted it to happen.

"I believe that you would never lie to me to make me feel better," she said with confidence. "So, yes, I believe you."

"Good. That's all that matters, alright? I'm not leaving you. I couldn't even if I tried, Gaia Wilson. When this is all done we'll have that talk I promised."

I went to kiss her forehead and she drew back, avoiding it.

"You can't kiss me when I have your—"

I snatched her back and pressed my lips right where I'd intended.

"I don't give a fuck about any of that. Whether your skin is covered in the blood of my mother or my enemy, I'll still kiss you, understood?"

"Understood," she murmured, burying herself in my chest. "I hope you know that you're also embedded in my heart, Ricardo Carter."

I'd know it well before she figured it out, but it was nice to hear that I didn't need to keep her here for another six weeks in order to win her heart.

It was time to get back to business as usual.

"Are your sisters upset?"

I led her over to the rolling chair and gently pushed her into it.

"At the moment, no. But you don't need to worry about that. Did you finish?"

She looked as if she wanted to argue but understood that we didn't have time for that and turned toward the computer.

"Yeah, it's a cheap system. I was able to destroy it pretty quickly. It's probably best to clear this whole room and make it look like the other private areas."

She glanced at me.

"If you want I can leak your father's affairs and the investigation into him to the media. I have a contact at the Washington Times who would jump at the chance to have this story before anyone else."

I nodded, liking the idea especially with my sister's staging for a murder-suicide.

There was a small detail I didn't plan on telling anyone but

Gaia about, but they'd understand after this was all said and done.

"You can reach out to your contact later. Ree and Ally want to handle their part alone and I want you to come with me. There's something else we need to do, but first, I want to get you home, showered, and changed. Everything we're wearing will have to be burned."

I stood and pulled her up.

As we were leaving, Ree and Ally's team were arriving.

If we didn't pull this off and I had to spend the rest of my life in jail to protect my sisters and the love of my life, I'd do it without complaint.

And in a fucking heartbeat.

CHAPTER 21

GAIA

he murder of the attorney general, followed by the suicide of his wife has sparked conversation across the nation this week. Is there—

The TV screen went black and I whipped my head around.

Rocco was already making his way over when my eyes met his.

"It's three in the morning and you're watching the news again," he complained. "Stop torturing yourself, Shortcake."

I pulled my legs to my chest and rested my head against my knees.

"I just wanted to know if there were any new developments."

He got down in front of me and pulled my legs from my chest, his fingers softly caressing the skin of my thigh in the process.

"Harlem is calling later to give us some news from one of his sources. No more CNN, okay?"

I nodded and slid to the end of the sofa.

"I've done a lot of crazy things but none of them have ever

made the news, not at this magnitude. This is... it's nerve wracking. I don't know how you're so calm when there have been camera crews parked outside all week."

They were relentless in their quest to get him to speak about his parents, but the FBI had instructed us to stay clear of doing interviews until the case had been fully investigated and concluded.

Rocco smiled and pulled us up.

"I grew up in the spotlight," he said, lifting me bridal style. "I'm used to having a camera or two in my face from time to time."

He carried me up the stairs instead of taking the elevator, taking his time while we talked.

I clung to him for support, not because I thought he'd drop me, but because my nerves were bad. It took a lot to keep my family from coming to D.C., but I couldn't expose them in that way.

Once Luci called my parents, because I refused, and they started seeing the news cycle my father wanted to come get me.

Rocco wouldn't allow it, insisting that I stay with him where I can be protected in his camera proof home.

I hadn't known the floor to ceiling windows were reflective. Someone trying to take pictures on the other side wouldn't capture anything but a black distorted void.

He'd drawn the automatic blinds a week ago and hadn't lifted them since.

Both of his sisters, who had decided to stay in their respective homes against Rocco's wishes, had the same kind of protective film on their windows.

"How are you feeling?" I asked as he entered his bedroom, dropped me gently on the bed and climbed in behind me.

"At peace," he murmured into my neck.

"But—"

"A lot happened that day," he went on, holding me tight. "Too much all at once but it happened and it's nothing either of us can do about it but leave it be."

I turned my body to face his, pressing myself closer.

Nose to nose, mouth to mouth, I said, "I want to know what you've been keeping from me."

Rocco's lips met mine and we shared a soft kiss.

"I told her that my father would make me..." He pressed his forehead to mine and sighed. "To toughen me up, he'd make me have sex with grown women and watch."

Horrified, I untangled myself from him and sat up.

"What?"

My heart raced.

How could... how could he do that to his son? Take his innocence away from him in such a disgusting and callous way.

Rocco sat up and braced himself on his hands.

"From eleven to fourteen," he went on. "It never felt right but I don't think I recognized what really happened to me until years later. In college, my relationships with women were fucked up. An accidental touch from someone random would make me flinch. It took a long time after that to snap out of it."

I climbed in his lap, straddling him.

"Ricardo, I am so sorry you had to experience that. I'm sorry no one protected you in the way you deserved."

"She didn't believe me," he said softly. "I told her and she in so many words called me a liar and told me not to slander his name in that way."

I cupped his face and waited for him to bring his eyes to mine.

Staring deeply at the man I loved with all my heart, I said, "I believe you."

He looked away and I said it again.

"I believe you. I believe you. I believe you."

When he found the courage to meet my unwavering gaze once more, his eyes were wet with tears.

"Thank you," he murmured, pulling me into his chest. "I knew if anyone would, it'd be you."

"Your truth will always be safe with me. You never have to worry about that."

I wiped away the few tears he let fall.

"It's safe here," I went on, kissing his forehead. "Your heart is safe with me, I hope you know that."

I was so fucking angry for him.

It pained me not to be able to bring his parents back to life and kill them all over again, this time slower and messier. Both deserved a messy death.

"I've been thinking about something," he said suddenly, frowning. "There was a lot going on and I thought the files from Valarie's would give some answers but all they did was prove she'd been doing under the table adoptions."

I nodded, already knowing this.

Had she not died, she would be spending the rest of her life in jail.

"So, what is it?"

"My father said my great aunt had given birth to twins, a girl—Lina, and a boy who was given to a friend of my grandfather."

I sat up.

"Holy shit. Do you think..."

I covered my mouth.

"Yeah..." Rocco nodded and laughed. "I think Angelo and Alina were twins."

He tapped my thigh and I got off him, sitting crossed

legged in the middle of the bed while he went into the closet and came back with a large book.

"I have some old pictures in here of Lina."

Rocco flipped through it and then sat down to show me.

His aunt, who was technically his second cousin, stood next to a younger Robert with the biggest smile on her face.

"She looked so happy," I mused.

"This was before my mother. They were probably..." He shook his head. "Can't believe they were like that with one another. He was defending her not being his sister, only for her to be his first cousin."

It was... a story that's for sure.

Shaking my head, I stared at the photo and started to see a resemblance between Lina and Angelo. They had the same nose and eyes. Their lips were even shaped the same.

I'd barely ever seen the former mafia boss smile but I had a feeling it would be identical to hers.

"There's only one way to really know if he's a Carter," I said. "But, we both know he won't take a DNA test."

"Yeah but Enzo and I could take one," Rocco said, glancing over. "I have a connect that could do it and then destroy our DNA from the system after the results are back."

Made men never willingly gave up their DNA, *ever.*

But this would close a chapter and open a new one for these two families.

Rocco would have a family who's already loved him properly since being in their lives.

"I think you've been with your family all this time," I murmured, smiling. "What a stroke of luck you ended up at the same college as Enzo and Matteo."

He chuckled.

"That's fucking crazy but I think we can safely say that this job is complete."

I twisted the heirloom I'd been wearing since he slid it on my finger.

"There's something else we need to talk about though..." I wiggled my fingers. "You asked me to think about it and the answer is yes, I will be your fiancée and later your wife."

He was exactly who I needed, the only safe haven that can protect my heart and soul from the craziness that comes with being in the mafia.

"Do you mean that?" he asked, setting the photo album aside.

I nodded and got off the bed to stand in front of him. Positioning myself between his legs, I wrapped my arms around his neck.

"I love you..." I shook my head. "No, I'm madly in love with you, Ricardo. Crazy in love. I'll kill a bitch over you in love. I want to be your wife."

He smiled and I'd gotten so used to seeing it reach his eyes that it didn't surprise me to see it this time either.

"I think that's the sweetest shit anybody has ever said to me."

He stood and turned us, pushing me on the mattress and tugging my legs apart.

"I love you," he murmured, settling between my thighs. "I'm insanely in love with you. It's deep and mad, but unconditional as fuck. I'd set the world on fire for you, Gaia Wilson. I'd burn just so the flames can't get to you. I want so badly to be your husband."

The lover girl in me swooned over his words.

"I can't wait to brag to my friends about how my man is a poet."

He chuckled and kissed my forehead.

"Don't tell them shit. You already got them calling me Ricardo, Shortcake."

I beamed at him.

"It's your name, baby."

"A name that's reserved for you and only you. You can't let them disrespect you like that."

I burst into laughter but sobered as his phone rang.

Rocco leaned over and grabbed it, swiping the screen to answer.

"What's up?"

"Turn the news on," I heard a voice that sounded a lot like Harlem say. "You're in the clear."

He set his phone aside and pulled me up, leading us downstairs to where the only TV was set up.

Rocco turned it on and flashing across the screen on CNN, while a video of the arrest of Avery Montrose by the FBI was playing, was a breaking news banner.

It read: *Avery Montrose, former attorney general's chief of staff, arrested for the murder of Robert and Deidre Carter.*

He turned the volume up.

It's said that the former chief of staff and late attorney general were having an affair," the analyst spoke, sharing a split screen of the arrest. *"What appeared to be a murder-suicide at first glance had been plotted by Avery Montrose to cover her tracks after what started as a lover's quarrel turned deadly. Reports from the Washington Times, lay out a detailed history of abuse from both parties. The FBI will be holding a press conference this afternoon to lay out the facts of the case."*

I smirked.

She'd been easy to frame.

The murder-suicide plot Ree and Ally had worked served its purpose, but when Rocco mentioned having something else to handle, I hadn't imagined breaking into her home to execute the real plan.

Now who's the criminal, Ms. Montrose?

I slept peacefully in Rocco's arms that morning after he dragged me back to bed, only waking to his soft kisses hours later.

"My sisters are on their way here," he murmured against my neck. "The lead investigator on the case reached out to inform them about the arrest and the press conference. We're still unsure of when they'll release the bodies for a funeral but I'm not in a rush for that."

There was still so much to wrap up but the hard part was over.

"We can take a shower together," I suggested, leaning into his kisses. "Save time and water."

"Mmhm," he hummed. "Sounds like a plan."

We'd wasted a lot of water doing everything but getting clean, but eventually got to the task we'd set out to do and showered. After dressing in longue clothes, I headed downstairs before Rocco who had stepped onto the terrace to take a call.

"Oh my... fuck," I shrieked, hand over chest after being startled by my father sitting at the island eating a fucking sandwich like he lived here. "Dad, what the hell?"

He looked up and smiled.

"Hey, Munchkin," he greeted. "Why isn't there any tomatoes? What's a sandwich without them?"

This fucking man.

"Dad..." I shook my head. "Ricardo is allergic to tomatoes. Why are you here?"

He pushed the plate aside and stood, approaching me slowly.

"Came to see the man you decided was more equipped to take care of you then me."

I sighed.

"I never said--"

"You didn't need to say it," Rocco said, entering the kitchen like he'd know my father was here the entire time. "He knows exactly what you meant, which is exactly what it is. You're mine to protect now, not his."

The two fucking psychos squared off, standing toe to toe.

"I cannot believe you two are doing this right now."

It was hard not to laugh because they were dead serious and there was nothing I could do about it.

"What kind of man is allergic to tomatoes?" my father asked, genuinely perturbed by it.

"That's what you want to know?" Rocco asked, tipping his head.

"It's what I asked, aint it?"

I walked around them and cleared the mess my dad made, deciding it was best to leave them to their... whatever the fuck they were doing.

Eventually, they migrated out of the kitchen to talk about whatever fathers and significant other's discussed. And before they returned, Ree and Ally arrived.

"Is someone else here?" Ally asked. "We saw a car out there we've never seen before."

I nodded.

"Yeah, my dad broke in and made a sandwich."

They burst into laughter and waved me off until my father and Rocco walked in.

It was the truth but I knew neither would believe me.

"Whoa, you're handsome," Ally complemented, covering her mouth after realizing she'd said it aloud.

My dad, unfazed by her comment, pulled me into a hug.

"We came to an agreement that when I visit tomatoes will be present," he said, kissing my forehead before staring in my eyes. "This is where you want to be, right?"

I nodded, loving him for understanding.

"Yes, it's where I want to be."

"And you'll come home to visit often?"

"Of course. How could I stay away from my favorite guy?"

"Aww," Ally cooed. "This is what we should've had."

I glanced at her but she was staring down at the island.

Her and Marie were playing unbothered about everything that transpired but I didn't believe it one bit.

"You shouldn't pretend not to be sad," dad said, addressing her. "It's okay to feel the loss of someone even if they were a piece of shit. He was your piece of shit."

He had no clue how to deliver a message better than that but I agreed with him.

Ally nodded.

"Did you really break in and make a sandwich?" she asked, already moving the conversation along.

"Wasn't that great of a sandwich," he replied, shrugging.

I slapped my forehead as they laughed, eyes meeting Rocco's across the room.

He gave a nod of reassurance and relief filled me.

My dad wasn't easy to please but he'd do anything for me, including accepting my boy--fiancé.

All was good in my world with his blessing.

CHAPTER 22
ROCCO

I rolled Gaia's bag to the elevator and dropped mine next to it.

We were heading back today and didn't plan on officially moving to D.C. until the summer. There was a bunch of shit happening that required our attention and attendance.

Violet and Finnegan were getting married in little over a week on Valentine's day.

Luca and Galina were only a few weeks away from her giving birth to their daughter, and their wedding would follow.

Gaia and I hadn't told anyone that we were engaged but wanted to marry in our own small ceremony before coming back.

"Dad, you can't just call dibs on a room and demand we not let anyone sleep in it," Gaia complained as she and her father stepped out the elevator together.

"Why not?"

He was an odd man, her father.

When we'd talked he didn't question me about intentions

or threaten me with bodily harm if I were to hurt her. His exact words were, *"If you're in her life then you're in mine. Don't try and change it, we're locked in now, Kid."*

It wasn't what I'd expected but watching him over the last few days I came to the realization that he was a man of action and expected the same from the person his daughter chose to be with.

He needed to see you be the person you claim to be, not hear you.

We had that in common.

"Because there are other people who might come visit," Gaia explained, hands on her hips.

"Munchkin, that has nothing to do with me," he said, turning in my direction. "Tell your fiancée you'll reserve my room."

I chuckled.

"How about we compromise and I build you and the wife an in-law suite?"

There was plenty of space to add in and I wasn't against accommodating the man.

"Ricardo, do not spoil him."

Xavier smiled.

"You'll get far in life, Son," he said, tossing an arm over Gaia's shoulder. "Nia will like you."

I was about to speak but the doorbell rang, which wasn't normal.

Anyone who came to my place, had a code to get in through the garage.

There wasn't a soul who would show up without me inviting them here first.

"I almost forgot there's a front door," Gaia said, following me to it.

Sliding the lock back, I pulled it open and frowned at the sight of Alice.

"It was you wasn't it?" she accused, taking a step forward.

Her clothes were disheveled, eyes red from crying.

I guess her mother's arrest was taking a toll but that wasn't my problem nor did I give a fuck about how it was affecting her.

"You did this, I know it. She would never--"

Gaia stepped around me before she could finish and clocked Alice in the face with a closed fist.

Her body jerked back from the impact but Gaia pulled her in, dragging her body down and halfway across the threshold. Kicking her leg over Alice's body, she dropped into a squat on her chest.

She ran her fingers along the inside of Alice's jacket, searching for a wire or listening device. After checking every inch of her, Gaia handed me her phone.

"Now, why would you think showing up here was okay?" she asked, fingers squeezing her neck.

"Y-You can't get away with it," Alice growled, flailing her body as best she could. "Get off of me you crazy bitch."

Gaia smiled and shook her head before slipping a blade from inside her sleeve.

I'd learned over the last few weeks that it was her favorite place to hide one.

"Didn't I tell you the last time we spoke that this isn't what you want? Now I have to prove a point."

She pressed the tip of the blade to Alice's cheek and slid it across the skin in one swift line.

"Ah!" Alice shrieked, swinging her head from side to side. "Stop. Stop."

I let Gaia get it out, allowing a few more strokes before stepping in.

"Let it rock, Shortcake. We have a flight to catch."

She looked up with her lip poked out.

"But, I was just getting started," she whined, widening her eyes to coerce me into letting her play for a little while longer. "She's trespassing on private property. I have a right to defend my home."

How Alice had gotten over the gate that led to my property was beyond me but Gaia was right, she was trespassing. And if she hadn't come to secretly record the conversation she wanted to force, then showing up here at all had been a big mistake.

"Munchkin, listen to your man," her father said, stepping forward.

He kneeled and brought his face close to Alice's, who flinched at the sight of his cold eyes.

"I don't know you," he stated calmly. "And you don't know me, but if I hear of you giving my daughter anymore trouble, it'll be me you'll have to see. I hate hurting women, so don't make me do it."

He stood and pulled Gaia up.

"Now go find some goddamn dignity," he instructed, waving her off. Your mother is a killer, plain and simple. The evidence says so."

Alice crawled across the threshold to the outside, holding her face with one hand to stop the bleeding.

"It's true," I lied, leaning in the doorway as she stood slowly. "The evidence speaks for itself. Maybe fucking the attorney general was her downfall. You should ask her about it. Don't come here again, the next time you won't leave at all."

I slammed the door and slid the lock in place.

"Now, I have to throw these out," Gaia complained," showing me the blood stained part of her sneaker.

"I'll buy five more pair to replace it."

She nodded and went to change her shoes, leaving me alone with her father.

"She has my temper," he mused, a proud look in his eyes. "Be grateful she has her mother's heart."

I was more than grateful for her kind heart but appreciated the parts of her father she'd inherited. It meant she wasn't somebody who could be bullied.

"I'm grateful for it all," I said, heading for the elevator as the doors opened and Gaia poked her head out.

"I'm ready now," she said.

We made it to the airstrip and was in the air in record time.

The flight going back felt shorter then when we'd left, but the tension wasn't the same.

"Oh, Ya, is here!" Gaia said, the biggest smile on her face as the flight attendant let the stairs down.

She raced to her cousin, Yasir.

He'd been leaning up against the passenger side of a black G-Class until he spotted her coming at him. Pushing off the door, he opened his arms for her and she jumped in them.

"Wassup, G," he greeted, spinning her around for a second before setting her on her feet. "You good?"

His gaze perused her frame to be sure, even though she'd nodded.

"I'm good..." She looked over her shoulder and smiled at me. "Yasir this is Rocco, my fiancé."

"Wassup, Rock," he said, calling me by the nickname people used on the streets. "You could have told me it was my cousin you wanted to pursue."

I shrugged.

Gaia glanced between us, frowning.

"Didn't know she was your cousin until recently."

"You two are talking like you know one another. What am I missing here?"

"Handled something for him way back when," I told her, leaving the details for him to provide if he chose to.

"Still owe you," he said, nodding.

"Nah..." I waved him off as Xavier approached. "We even now."

Her father gripped my shoulder to get my attention.

"Stop by and have dinner this week," he demanded. "Nia is expecting the both of you."

I nodded.

He kissed Gaia on the cheek, opened the passenger door, and got in.

"Let's go, Ya," he called before closing it.

"This muthafucka think I'm his chauffeur," Yasir grumbled with a smirk. "Might drop his ass off on the side of the road."

He tipped his head at me and ruffled Gaia's mane.

"Later, G."

They pulled off and Gaia turned to regard me.

"Can't believe you know my cousin."

I shrugged and rolled her bags to my Camaro.

Enzo had one of the guys pick it up when we left and drop it off upon our arrival.

"I know a lot of people..." I opened her door. "Get in."

After she was in her seat, I shut the door and loaded our bags.

"Are we going to Enzo's first?" she asked as I slid into the driver's seat.

"Yeah, we'll stay in Jersey tonight and your place tomorrow."

"What about after that?"

"Doesn't matter. Pick a place and that's where we'll be."

I reached over and caressed her thigh for a second and then settled it between her legs where it was nice and warm.

"We can look for a new place to share for when we're in town," I offered. "Somewhere between everyone."

"Not anything too big though. Your spot in D.C. is our home."

It felt good hearing her say that.

"*Our* spot," I corrected. "You can make changes if you want. Switch up the decor, I don't care. Just want you to feel like it's yours too."

"My plant babies will have to be relocated," she mused to herself. "I love plants."

They were all over her townhome, hanging, on tables, and shelves.

I mentally planned out building her a greenhouse during our ride to the casino.

Whatever she wanted, she could have.

The hour it took getting to Enzo's had knocked Gaia out and for a short while I watched her sleep instead of waking her.

She always looked so damn peaceful and I hated disturbing it.

"Baby," I called softly, stroking her cheek. "We're here."

She stirred a little and whined.

"One more minute," she murmured, brushing her forehead against my arm. "So soft."

I chuckled.

"I thought you were excited to hold baby Enzo. Guess, I'll just have to leave you in here and—"

She popped up. "Oh, you meant were *here*."

Wiping her eyes, she beamed at me.

"Come on," she ordered as if that hadn't been what I was trying to do. "I've been missing my cuddles with his little face."

We entered through the apartment side and headed up to the top floor where Enzo and Lucia lived. The elevator opened into their place and everyone was there, waiting for us it seemed.

"Damn," I deadpanned, looking around after Gaia released my hand. "Y'all missed us this bad?"

"So much," Matteo droned from his spot in the kitchen.

Akira was sitting next to him, eating a fucking orange, while Gianna who wasn't with her husband Cian, stood on the other side of the island smiling.

Enzo and Lucia came from the back and Gaia took off in their direction.

"Give me the baby and we won't have any problems," she threatened halfheartedly.

"The parents matter, too," Lucia complained, while doing exactly as Gaia asked and handing little man over.

Her eyes met mine as I dropped down on the sofa and lifted my boot on the coffee table.

"Ricardo, remove your shoes from my table."

I dropped them after she asked, smiling in her direction.

"Can we not call him by his government name, thanks," Gaia said, coming to sit next to me.

I watched her dote on her baby cousin, wondering how many kids she'd be willing to give me in the future.

"You got something you wanted to tell us?" Enzo asked, drawing my attention to where he'd sat across the room.

Gaia squeezed my knee gently and I appreciated the support.

Before heading back, I'd told him it was best he brought Matteo and Gianna in to hear what I found together. Only the three of them could deliver the news to their father.

"We need to confirm this with a DNA test, but I'm almost certain the three of you are technically my third cousins."

Enzo didn't react but I expected nothing less from him. He

wasn't the type to show what he was thinking until he felt like it.

"Wait..." Lucia walked from the kitchen to the living room. "That would mean your father was Angelo's first cousin."

I nodded, breaking down how we'd come to this conclusion.

By the time I finished, Matteo and Gianna were standing in the living room too.

"So, dad was a twin?" Gianna asked, shaking her head. "Whoa."

I pulled out the few pictures of my au—cousin and handed them to Matteo.

"I see the resemblance," he said, handing them to Gianna who then gave them to Enzo.

He flipped through the pictures slowly and then looked at me.

"You've been our blood family all this time," he finally said.

I nodded.

"My guy can test us to confirm," I offered. "It'll be discreet and destroyed afterward."

"You guys have always been family," Gaia said, looking between the four of us. "I'm grateful that he had you."

It made all these years having only them to depend on that much better.

"Is there something else we should know?" Gianna asked, scrutinizing us. "You two seem closer than usual."

I noticed Akira, who had stayed in the kitchen, peek around Matteo with a little smile on her face.

"That's because we are," Gaia said without pause. "Plus, I'm gonna be a wife soon."

She lifted her left hand and wiggled her fingers to show off the ring.

"Yes!" Akira cheered, winking at me. "I knew you had it in you."

She was a fucking character but I liked her.

The girls were checking out the ring and I stood, nodding for Enzo and Matteo to meet me in the kitchen.

"Remember the deal we made?" I asked, looking between them.

"Whenever you want out we'd award that to you no questions asked," Matteo said while Enzo watched me.

I nodded.

"Here's the thing..." I leaned into the counter. "I don't want out, but I do want in on the expansion."

They looked at one another.

It had always been the plan to infiltrate D.C. when my father was out of office. Now that his time had been cut short, it was the perfect opportunity.

"I have the connections," I went on. "I've outgrown being the family's enforcer."

Enzo nodded.

"We think so, too," he agreed. "How about Capo of D.C.? It's yours if you want it."

Moving up in rank and having my own territory to run wouldn't be easy but I was bred to do it.

"Yeah..." I looked over at Gaia, who was smiling from ear to ear. "I want it."

And I had the perfect partner to execute my new found position flawlessly.

Just so happened she was gonna be my wife one day.

Who was going to stop us?

EPILOGUE

Gaia

It was the day before Finnegan and Violet's wedding and we were all in New York staying on his parent's estate. Knowing the O'Sullivan's were loaded and seeing it was another thing.

The men were staying separate from the women but Ricardo had insisted on me sneaking out to see him like we were teenagers, like I wasn't a grown ass woman who moved around as she pleased.

But did I wait until the girls had fallen asleep to meet my man in the garden?

Of course.

"Where are you taking me?" I asked, trying to keep up with his long strides.

He pulled me behind a large hedge and kissed me, his fingers slipping into my shirt to cup my bare breasts. My body lit up from his touch, awakening an ache between my legs I needed quelled as soon as possible.

"Where's your bra?" he asked, pulling back to lift my shirt and expose me. "Pretty ass nipples.

Before I could respond, his lips were wrapped around the hardened buds and a mixture of pain and pleasure burst through me as he tugged and sucked on them, giving each an equal amount of attention.

I could barely hold myself up.

He was insatiable, a goddamn fiend.

"I fucking need you," he growled, snatching me forward to spin me around. "Can I have you right here, Shortcake?"

I pressed my ass into him and bent over, pulling at my leggings to get them down to my ankles.

There were no words needed.

He was inside of me faster than I could blink, pulling me into his chest by my neck while fucking me from behind hard and fast.

"Baby," I cried, meeting his relentless strokes. "Don't stop."

I hadn't realized how much I needed him inside of me until this very moment.

We were spending our first valentine's day together, celebrating our friends.

And while I was honored to be here, because I loved Violet something bad, I loved my man just a little more.

"Couldn't let this day start without telling you happy first Valentine's day," he murmured softly in my ear while stroking my pussy slow. "I love you."

His heart was so pure and I couldn't feel happier that I got to witness it in real-time.

"I love you," I moaned, hooking my arm around to touch his face.

We fucked leisurely, like we had all the time in the world to be out here.

My body held on for as long as it could, but the sensation

dancing in my core became so overwhelming that I couldn't keep myself together anymore.

Everything poured out of me onto his dick.

"Damn, baby..." He pushed his fingers between my legs and stroked my clit, wounding me up again. "This pussy so wet. So good."

I bent forward and grabbed my ankles before rocking back into him.

He grabbed my waist and dug into me, rearranging my insides in the best kind of way.

I tightened my walls around his dick and he cursed, pulling me into his body as he halted his strokes and came.

"Goddamn, woman," he breathed, keeping me in place.

I smiled at the ground like a fucking fool.

Pussy wet, ass in the air, and the dick still buried inside of me.

A bitch was proud.

"It's all over my inner thighs," I murmured, sticking my fingers in my essence.

Rocco lowered himself and pushed my legs apart.

"Lemme clean you up, baby."

He covered my pussy with his mouth and sucked, slurping my juices until there was nothing left.

What a fucking man.

As he stood, he pulled my leggings up, adjusted himself, and then took my hand.

"I'll walk you back."

We moved through the silence in less hurried steps than when we came out.

In front of the guest house at the right side of the property, he kissed me slow and sweet, stirring up my insides again.

"Happy valentine's day," he muttered against my lips.

"Happy valentine's day to you," I murmured back, wrapping my arms around his neck.

I didn't want him to leave but eventually he forced me to go inside.

Resting against the door, I smiled.

"Nasty," Violet said, walking toward me from the kitchen with a knowing smirk on her face.

Busted.

"What are you doing up?"

She shrugged and dropped down on the sofa.

"I'm used to sleeping with Finn. Didn't realize how bad I needed him for a decent nights rest."

I nodded.

"It's a shame how bad we've got it."

She smiled and it lit up her face.

"Yeah, but they've got it bad, too. We can call it even."

I went into the kitchen and washed my hands before sitting on the other end of the sofa.

"I'm happy for you," I told her. "You've always deserved to have that content expression on your face. I don't think I've ever seen you smile so big before."

"Don't get all sappy on me, Gaia," she warned, her lips curling into a smirk. "You know how much I hate it."

I chuckled.

"Yeah but I had to tell you anyway."

She nodded and our eyes met.

"Thank you for being my family all these years."

"Now who's being sappy?"

She laughed and stood, stretching.

"Fucking Finn turned me into a half lover girl or whatever," she said, rolling her eyes. "But, I don't know. Feels good..." She shrugged. "I'm going to try and get some sleep. You should, too."

I watched her disappear into the main bedroom and smiled.

Damn, we've come a long way.

Later that day, after we watched Violet marry her soulmate, I couldn't help but think about my own impending ceremony. Rocco and I had decided on a smaller wedding but big enough for our circle.

I envisioned different ideas and concepts over and over but the one thing that remained the same was the man I loved standing at the top of the aisle waiting to make me his by law.

"Can't wait to make you my wife," Ricardo murmured into the skin of my neck as we slow danced. "I can't wait to be your husband."

"I can't wait to be your wife," I whispered back. "To make you my husband."

Whatever became of that day, he was all that mattered.

The safest place in the world for me.

The protector of my heart and soul.

My sinful enforcer.

AUTHOR NOTES

Thank you for reading.
I hope you enjoyed the sixth book in the Mafia Misfits series.
Please leave me a review on Amazon and/or Goodreads.
Interested in viewing a Pinterest board with visuals from the book?
Link: https://pin.it/Ib7V1Ol
Would you like to read bonus content from the series? Join my Patreon here: patreon.com/asiamonique
Here are a few ways to stay connected with me:
Website: www.asiamonique.com
Like me on Facebook: http://bit.ly/AuthorAsiaMonique
Join my readers group on
Facebook: http://bit.ly/ForTheLoveOfAsiaMonique
Follow me on TikTok: https://vm.tiktok.com/TTPdkpVDvK/
Follow me on Instagram: www.instagram.com/_ayemonique

Made in the USA
Columbia, SC
27 November 2024

47725449R00157